STARDUST
TURNS TO
Love

STARDUST TURNS TO *Love*

THE GOLDEN THREAD THAT BINDS

CARA CARÓN

MILL CITY PRESS

Mill City Press, Inc.
2301 Lucien Way #415
Maitland, FL 32751
407.339.4217
www.millcitypress.net

Paperback ISBN-13: 978-1-66283-506-3
Ebook ISBN-13: 978-1-66283-507-0

Acknowledgements

To all those souls
who believe dreams do come true
and are creating their reality

God gave us the gift of life;
it is up to us to give ourselves
the gift of living well
…Voltaire

TABLE OF CONTENTS

Chapter 1

ANTONIO COMES TO NICE

*R*elaxing down by the water, Ann reminisced. My thoughts were remembering how Egidio loved me completely and how glad I am that I moved to France. We had a dream life and I always feel warm and fuzzy when I remember him. I'll never be certain what caused his demise, but nothing will bring him back. I now have to take over the Durand Yacht company here in Nice.

Antonio is incredibly special to me. He knew Egidio much longer than me, and I love him for him always being there for me and I know he loves me as he did Egidio. It seems I never thought of Antonio as a partner in our business or in life as Egidio filled all my needs. I am attracted to Antonio. It feels like I'm having an affair

1

on Egidio, although I know he would be happy for me if I were happy. The business is flourishing now that Antonio agreed to come and take over. He and I have got the finances under wraps. He is moving to Nice this week into his own apartment. He wanted to be close to the marina, so he could watch over the guys at the dock. We do have a manager Andre, but Antonio and I like to be hands on.

Antonio came strolling down the path to the water and sat down on the wicker chair next to me.

"Ann, The Inspiration, our favorite yacht really needs some pizazz for the clients next week. They are having some friends to celebrate their wedding anniversary. They have huge requests, or I should say requirements," Antonio quipped.

"Antonio, please get me the list so I can start working on it as soon as possible. There are two other yacht clients I am working with now; it's a stretch."

The week went quickly and Antonio's moving day arrived. He was moving back from Monaco. He didn't have a lot of things to move as the apartment was fully furnished. He had some great pieces of art, and some statues he had collected from places he had traveled. He had great taste and I had similar. We seem to match hand in glove about most things.

"Antonio where am I going to get these things from their list?"

"Andre has been with Durand since before Egidio had taken over the company. When I came on board Andre decided to stay. He is like a detective finding all the specialty items that your clients demand. Andre has a partner Claud who works with him and books the private planes to deliver requests to our yachts. Give him a call and I'm fairly sure he will be able to fill your requests." Antonio said.

"I never in my wildest thoughts figured I would be in the business of chartering these yachts. When I decided to marry Egidio, I only planned on being a support system for him. When he passed, I was in for more than I signed up for. I now enjoy refurbishing the yachts, but these clients seem to think they own us and in some ways they do. I am glad Antonio that you decided to come on board." Ann said.

"Ann, you know I love you and I will do anything to help you in the business as well as to help you personally." Antonio said.

"I have been thinking about giving Andre a raise and putting him in charge of dealing with the clients requests. Andre has a special way with women. They seem to think he is a demi-God. Of course, it makes our life that much easier. In fact, I'll call him right now. I don't know why it took me so long to come up with that idea. If I have to say so myself, the idea is genius. Sometimes I think these women ask for things just to see if we will come through. If they challenge Andre, they woke up the wrong tiger. He cannot deal with defeat, at any cost or idea, he will conquer. Antonio, I cannot seem to reach Andre; do you know where he is today?" Ann asked.

"No, I don't, but Andre has a new lady friend on the other side of Nice. Her name is Gabrielle. He sneaks off to see her every so often. One thing about Andre all said and done, he gets the job done. We really need him so we can continue to be the best. Durand Charters has always been number one in the yacht arena. Andre has been a huge part of keeping it that way for years. Egidio's father hired Andre as a young guy. I think he saw Andre's talent early on. He has such a way with people, he can tell them to go to hell and they don't know they were hit. Not many people have that gift. One thing about him he has always been a ladies' man. He was married for a short time; they tell me when he was young. They say he was always a stud but couldn't keep his pants zipped. His wife left. Ever since that he seems to have a collection of women to draw from. He is so charismatic; his curly black hair and his big blue eyes draw most of his women. All we need to know that his charm satisfies our clients," Antonio quipped.

"I will give him a call tomorrow. Right now, I have this obnoxious client, Ms. Balencia who thinks she owns the yacht. She has looked through the binders of all six of our yachts. She has something to say derogatory about each of them. She must own the Botox company.

When I was at my wits end, I suggested she might want to go with a different yacht company. Ann said.

"Her father owned a bra company in Marseilles, and she got the company and all his wealth when he passed. Egidio knew him. He said that the man was humble. Marcy Balencia wanted to marry Egidio, but he said he was never interested." Antonio mentioned.

"Ms. Balencia said to me, "Are you just trying to get rid of me, or do you want my business? I said, you will make that decision. After that she settled down when she knew she couldn't get my goat. We now are on good business terms. She decided to pick, Bonne Chance, our most expensive yacht. I can't wait to see what her demands will be so that she can be the queen. I'm expecting that Andre can handle her. I'm sure it would take someone like Andre to beat her down without her knowing she had been hit. Good thing only you and I, Antonio are having this discussion. Little do our clients know that we hold the upper hand. I often think that many of those people come from old money. Generally, our clients that have always had money seem to treat us much better." Ann said.

Antonio went to the marina to check on things. When he came back, I had just got off the phone.

"Well, I got a hold of Andre, and he was thrilled that now with his new title he would be getting paid for what, for the most part he was always doing. He thanked me with a little smirk on his face. I just thought he was being cute." Ann said.

Antonio and I were getting closer and closer. He is such a great guy, and he tells me he always loved me since he met me but respected Egidio and knew his place. He said never in his wildest dreams did he think we would ever be together.

"Ann, be careful. Andre is a ladies' man, who has no bounds. You have money and now you're a widow. You are a prime target for men. I owe it to Egidio to look out for you being he is no longer around." Antonio said.

"Marcy Balencia wants an Africa theme for one night. I will need to put fabric on the walls that are some of the leopard skins and zebra skins. You know we've always gathered those from dead animals. We've never killed animals to get those skins. I guess you know that. We do, in the warehouse have some monkeys that were finished by a taxidermist that we can suspend from the ceilings. We also have a lot of greenery to create the jungle look. The crew coming in for this trip will arrange all the dining. The client's request is that the crew other than the captain, wear African garb. I know they won't go for that, but they do need their jobs.

Ms. Balencia wants to book another trip in June. That trip is to reflect the 1700's in Europe. All guests are to be in formal attire. The ladies in ball gowns and all wear wide brimmed hats. Where to store these hats is the question; they take up a lot of space. All the ball gowns will need to be properly pressed. All artwork is to be French or Russian." Ann explained.

Chapter 2

ASTRID VISITS

"There is a girl I met quite some time ago on one of the crews. Her name is Astrid. She is from Sweden, and she seems to be on call for all European requests from clients. She and I became friends and when there is a yacht coming into Nice, she and I get together. We have many of the same interests. I enjoy her company and she always has some unbelievable stories from on board. She is travelling on both charters for "Her Majesty", Ms. Balencia." Ann said.

"Ann, I think we need a night away. I am inviting you to go to Le Chantecler for dinner tonight." Antonio suggested.

"Mon Coeur, I totally agree. I would enjoy spending a night with us, no work talk, to enjoy each other's company. Sometimes it's hard to know where Andre is coming from. Most of the time I just ignore his remarks because they seem inappropriate to me." Ann said.

"Ann, you are so beautiful and kind, any man would be attracted to you as am I. Just be careful, his reputation goes before him."

We arrived at the restaurant at eight. As per usual, Antonio knew the chef and he immediately seated us. I had been there before and always enjoyed their plates with the roosters on them, their trademark. Their presentations were always superb, a work of art. It was late so Antonio stayed over. He stayed in the guestroom that night. Somehow, I still had times when I felt like I was cheating on Egidio, Antonio would pick up on that and stay in the guestroom. He has been wonderfully considerate of my feelings.

Monday seemed to arrive soon. I went down to the dock and checked in with the fellows at the Marina. There were two yachts going out on the same day. It was a scramble to see to it that every detail had been attended to. Andre appeared and his usual self were remarks, I thought were uncalled for. He put his arm around me and kidded me to say, "Ann, you are one sensitive lady. A little hug now and then is good for what ails you." I brushed his arm off my shoulder.

"Andre, even a little kid knows, keep your hands on your own body."

I left to go down to the dock. Astrid was coming in on one of the charters. I was looking forward to catching up with her. She is a yachtie on several yachts. I invited her to stay with me for a few days. She always had many good stories to tell of the clients on the charters. She certainly in her job was not allowed to share stories with crewmembers or supposedly other people. She and I had a personal relationship. She knew I would not share stories because I own yachts.

I drove down to the pier to meet Astrid and we decided to go out to lunch. We decided to go to Le Canon. It is reminiscent of an ancient wine cave, with wine bottles adorning the walls.

This day, Astrid had a myriad of stories. "This last one was the guest request dining al fresco, not by the water, but in the water. We had to get floating tables and set breakfast off in a bay. All was fine until a thunderstorm rolled in." Astrid said.

We laughed so hard and then she told me this one. "One time we were in the Caribbean and near St. Bart's. This crazy guest decided they had to have bagels from Zabar's in New York for the next day. We had to get a private jet to fly them in; the pilots had to taxi them to the yacht. Another yacht trip, this brazen millionaire insisted the chef put peanut butter on the branzino."

"What in the world is branzino?" Ann asked.

"Branzino is European Seabass. The chef said no. He then suggested, he would serve it on the side. The guest spread the peanut butter all over the fish as if it were bread." Astrid said.

At this point we had drunk enough wine and then our entrée came. We each looked at each other and didn't know if we wanted to eat after the Seabass story.

"Astrid, I'm glad you could stay for a few days. I am constantly working with men and its refreshing to have some feminine conversation."

"I want to go today to Lea boutique. I heard they have some exceptional dresses. I don't get to dress much because on the yachts we must wear our uniforms. If we stop in a port, most of us are too tired after dealing with these obscene requests, we want to go to sleep." Astrid said.

"Let's go back to my place, go to the pool and have some lavender water. Tonight, Antonio is going to spend the evening with his friend, Alessandro. They met in Italy. They both are avid sailors. Antonio's sailboat will accommodate six guests. They are talking about going out to some island for a week or two. You and I will have the whole night to ourselves. I think I will have Collette, my housekeeper make up a few sandwiches for us this evening. We can sit down by the water at the gazebo, watch the sunset and relax."

"Ann, it's always great to be here. It's peaceful and I enjoy your company." Astrid said.

The time went so quickly, and the next day Astrid had another assignment. She left early in the afternoon. Antonio came in.

Chapter 3

ANTONIO HAS AN IDEA

"Ann, do you think we could go to dinner tonight? I've had a busy day and I'm sure you have too. I have some ideas I would like to run past you. Alessandro and I had a long talk last night. I would really like to know your thoughts on our ideas," Antonio said.

"I have two yachts going out this week and each one has extreme requests for the interiors. Each one is an extreme for me to carry out everything that these special guests, or crazy as I think of them, want me to accomplish." Ann said.

"Ann, you have been giving your life to this company. I feel you are still trying to fill your time, so you don't have to deal with the loss of Egidio. Please come out with me tonight." Antonio said.

"Antonio, as much as I would like to dispute what you said, I feel you hit the nail on the head. Yes, for sure, let's go to dinner."

"Let's go to La Terrasse in Le Méridien Hotel. I happen to know the maître d' there. François and I have gone sailing together. It is peaceful and we can overlook the water. Might I suggest the Salmon Fume or the Foie Gras Terrine. After dinner, we can take a little walk along the water. "Antonio suggested.

Antonio is just the ticket for me now. He is always concerned about my well-being. He never lets me pick up the check, although I would. We, I need to remember are just enduring friends so far. It seems to work best that way. I am thankful that he is helping me with Durand. No way could I handle all this myself. We well have all bases covered now. We have upped our pricing to the value of what we give to the clients. Most clients have never complained about the cost, but some of them although they have a great amount of money, still think this is, "Let's Make a Deal." Antonio is a great businessman and what I cannot come up with he can.

As soon as we arrived for dinner, François was gracious and he said to Antonio, "My man you sure have outclassed yourself with this beautiful woman."

"François, I'd like to introduce you to Ann."

"Enchante, François." Ann said.

He immediately seated us at the window overlooking the sea. The sky was cerulean blue with puffy white clouds, the sea was calm and all was well with the world. Antonio was right. I needed this night away and to be spending it with him was a pleasure. Antonio ordered a bottle of Bordeaux and let the night begin. Antonio ordered the Salmon, and I took his suggestion and ordered the Foie Gras. We both agreed not to have dessert, but to go out to a table near the water and sip a Frangelico. It was such a pleasant evening as there was a slight breeze and the gentle sound of the sea.

"Ann, Alessandro and I would like to take a trip and get my sailboat out on the water. We were thinking of being gone about a week or two later in the year. We would consider taking Claud as our man to tend to any problems with the sailboat. I was thinking before that we might take a vacation together, you and I." Antonio suggested.

"Where did you have in mind? I would like to go where there would be nice sandy beaches, not too many tourists and of course we need fine cuisine, being you are in the business." Ann said.

Chapter 4

TRAVEL TO ST. LUCIA

"I was thinking of St. Lucia. I have been there before because it's one of the best places to dive and I would enjoy that. You may not dive, but I do think you would enjoy snorkeling. I thought now to plan a trip. We could leave as soon as we are out of high season." Antonio said.

"I have never been there, but I'm anxious to leave for vacation in two weeks, I should be able to arrange with Andre and his team to run this place for a few weeks. I think we should stop in New York because the trip is long. It would break it up and I haven't seen my mother for so long. Once she sold the house, she moved to New York. Antonio, what do you think of us seeing a few

Broadway plays while we're there and then continue on to St. Lucia?" Ann queried.

"Great idea Ann and once we set the dates, I will look into which plays are on Broadway at that time. Matter of fact, I'll Google it right now. Looks like you and I might enjoy, Chicago and the Lion King."

"Antonio, how did you know those are two of my favorites. You are such a mind reader, that's what I love about you. On many things we think alike."

The night waned and we walked along the water and Antonio wanted to stay with me this night. I felt close to him and felt his love for me. We got home about 2 am and Antonio came out of the bathroom with only his tall slender perfect body. His body enhanced by his dark hair. I was about to have an orgasm right there. I slid into bed and felt his warm body next to mine. His hands were warm and tender as he kissed my breasts. The temperature was rising in both of us. He whispered words of love and entered gently. We fell asleep in each other's arms.

Morning came quickly, and I had to come back to earth and tend to business but, I was excited about the trip and also being able to see Mom. I had to call her.

"Mom it's Ann. I have a surprise to tell you about. Antonio and I have decided to take a vacation together to St. Lucia, but that's not the surprise. The surprise is that we are going to stop off in New York and we want to stop at your apartment. If it's all right with you, we will stay over a few nights and if you like you can go with us to see either Chicago or Lion King."

"Ann, I am ecstatic. I will be very glad to see you. I've been lonesome since your dad died. It sounds like you and Antonio have consummated your relationship, as I only have two bedrooms you know."

"Oh mother, you always say the silliest things. Of course, the answer is yes and I'm sure you could have surmised that without asking." Ann said.

"Just sayin', I may be old school, but I guess your grandmother was not. You know I love you and know you can make your own decisions," Mom said.

"In all my excitement, I forgot to ask how things are going for you. I guess though, we talked last week so I know. I must run now as one of the yachts is going out today. I will call you with details as soon as I know. Love you Mom, bye."

The time passed quickly. Antonio made all the arrangements, and we were headed for the airport. We had to be prepared because there is a seven-hour time difference between Nice and New York City. Antonio is so agreeable that I knew traveling with him would be a non-issue.

We finally arrived in New York and Mom picked us up at the airport. She had not met Antonio. I introduced them and as I suspected they both were congenial, and I knew the stay would be pleasant. That evening, Antonio suggested we go to dinner at La Cirque as he knew the Chef, Jacque. Antonio had been trained by him at the Italian Chef Academy in Rome, Italy. The walls had an ecru background and black sketches of monkeys swinging all over them.

That night the three of us were seated at the Chef's table. Chef Jacque was thrilled to reconnect with Antonio. Jacque couldn't say enough about Antonio's culinary skills. Mom was a bit overwhelmed. She hesitated to disturb the beauty of the presentation. She didn't want to disturb the arrangement. Antonio was comforting to her. He told her to enjoy herself and if necessary, he would re-create the plate. Mom just laughed and then smiled at Antonio's charisma.

The next evening, we went to see Lion King at the Minkoff theatre. The production was terrific. The giraffes walked through the audience, performers on stilts. All three of us had an outstanding time.

The next evening, we went to dinner at Sign of the Dove. The plating was creative. Each plate was a work of art. The walls were hung with European art pieces.

We then went over to the Ambassador Theatre to see Chicago. The cast and the characters were entertaining. The vocalists were dramatic. The lights of Broadway were stunning. Mom wasn't used to this kind of lifestyle.

When we arrived back to Mom's, we talked to the wee hours. Our flight the next day to St. Lucia was at 10 AM. Mom drove us to the airport. We cried and hugged and said our goodbyes.

I think Antonio had really had enough of girl talk, but he was understanding and kind. Antonio had lost both of his parents early on and he knew how important family is to someone. I hadn't known about Antonio's trauma until this trip. He never talked about it. When we got on the plane, I asked him about it. He was hesitant to talk, but he felt he owed it to me to share. His parents were getting ready to go on a vacation, they were on their way to the airport when a semi rolled over, and their car slid under and killed both. Antonio said to this day, the pain is fresh, less often but painful. He said that's why he doesn't talk about it. We needed to enjoy this vacation of ours and I thanked him for suggesting the trip.

As we got off the plane, a van was waiting for us. The hotel was quite a distance, so we had to go through the rain forest to get to our hotel. We got to the hotel in St. Lucia about 3 o'clock. It was a gorgeous hotel named Les Sport.

After we identified our luggage, the bellman said he would take it up to our room. We checked in and went to the bar and each had a piña colada. After that we took our shoes off and walked in the sand along the beach. It had been a long day, we decided to take a short nap. Antonio was a little frisky at first but was soon fast asleep.

We woke about 5 o'clock and decided to go to the front desk. I made a reservation for dinner for the following evening. We decided for this night just to get some pizza and a drink and bring it to our room. After pizza, Antonio reached for my hand and guided me right to our bed.

"You are easy to be with my Ann. Your long black, silky hair becomes you. You are pretty; you take my breath away. Lie down and let me feast my eyes on your alluring body."

Next morning, we went to breakfast. A delightful array of papaya, mango and pineapple were served. After breakfast, Antonio went down to the water to the scuba hut and signed up for their next dive. He had his certification and he had brought along his dive mask. The fellow at the desk told him to be at the water tomorrow morning at seven.

Antonio decided to go sit out by the pool and read awhile. I decided to go up to the spa in the afternoon. One had to follow the walkway and then there were three levels of stone stairs and at the top is where the spa was located. I signed up for the seaweed wrap and the following day for a full body massage.

Antonio was gone early the next morning, before I got up. My reservations at the spa were for 1 o'clock and 3 o'clock.

The water was perfect this morning. No waves just calm water, sky was blue with white puffy clouds. Antonio had gone down to the water to meet the diving group.

I got up, put my swimsuit on and my wrap and went to breakfast. I couldn't get enough papaya or mango. I sat overlooking the pristine white sand and the lapping turquoise waves. It was breathtaking. I needed this time of relaxation. We had the penthouse suite, and it had its own private hammam and gorgeous views.

When Antonio came back, he told me what the diving instructor said, "All of you people line up and I will break you into pairs of two. You must always stay with your dive partner. Today I want you to get into the water and then put your fins on. Make sure you check your gear. We are going to the coral reefs, and I repeat you must stay with your buddy." Antonio said.

We both went to the pool and Antonio fell asleep in one of the shaded chairs. I swam for quite a while and then relaxed in the beach chair.

Dinner was at eight at the Chateaubriand. All meals were French service. The presentation was exquisite. Antonio was impressed, that says a lot being he is a Michelin Chef. We began with champagne to celebrate our first vacation. The ambiance was enhanced by secluded lighting everywhere. The palm trees had mini white lighting twisted around the trunks. They sparkled at night.

One day, we decided to snorkel. We had to borrow equipment as we didn't bring our own. The fish were so colorful, blues, yellows and orange, like I had never seen.

Antonio about lost me, I got carried away. One loses space and time with all the underwater beauty.

Next day we took a hike up to Pigeon Point. It was a panoramic view. In the afternoon we went with a guide into the rain forest and saw different species of birds and wildflowers. An enlightening day and an exhausting one. We tried fried plantains and a lot of rum and went to the buffet that evening. We retired early as our flight was at eight in the morning, we had to take the van very early.

Chapter 5

ANTONIO PLANS THE TRIP

We arrived back to Nice and were totally wore out. We got to know each other better with traveling together. I found Antonio does have a short fuse. He likes everything to go perfect and of course nothing does. If needed, I have the patience of a saint. Antonio is quite different from Egidio in that, Egidio would need a firecracker put under to get him upset. Both personalities would need a little adjusting, to come to center. I couldn't believe the beauty of the fish when I snorkeled. Snorkeling was a brand-new experience for me. Now, every trip I would take, I would want to snorkel if it was available. I was thinking back over my life, from where it started to where I am now and there is no way if you would have told me how it would unfold, that I would believe you. But here I am, living my new life in France and enjoying every minute.

Collette had prepared dinner the night after we came back. She had made her special bread recipe and Manicotti. After dinner, I suggested Antonio and I would walk down to the water, through the garden paths and past the fountain.

"Antonio let's sit here in the gazebo for a minute." We sat in the swing together.

"Antonio, I have a proposition for you. I think you should come live with me and give up paying for your apartment. You spend more time here than at home. What is your thought?" Ann suggested.

"I have thought about it for a while but didn't know how to approach the situation. I want to so I could spend more time with you and not have to go home."

"Let's do it then. You don't have a contract so, at the end of the month, come live with me."

We agreed. My house was paid for so we could share the other expenses. Antonio and I were on the same page.

Antonio was back to planning his trip with Alessandro and wanted to ask Andre if he could spare Claud for a few weeks.

"Ann, I am going down to the marina this afternoon to see Andre. Always seemed Andre ruled with an iron hand. I realized it is better to approach Andre rather than talk to Claud." Antonio said.

When Antonio came back after dinner time, he seemed rather upset.

"Andre knew I would be coming in to ask if Claud could be spared. Andre and Claud were in the office in a deep conversation. I could hear them from outside arguing with each other. Claud kept hollering, "I don't want to, I don't want to." When I came in, Claud stormed out. I talked to Andre about leaving Claud go on my sailing venture. He grumbled and grumbled, but finally agreed." Antonio said.

Antonio came in the kitchen. "Ann, I apologize to you with all my heart. I know you already ate dinner. Andre and I had a long, long conversation. He wasn't thrilled to let Claud come with Alessandro and me for that length of time. Claud has always had a series of black clouds over his head. His wife died in childbirth. His mother raised his daughter as he had to work to support her. Next his mother passed suddenly. He wants calm at any cost, he agrees with everybody except with Andre today. After several glasses of Calvados, Andre agreed to let Claud go with us.

Ann, I don't know if you know much about Andre's personal life. He has some serious issues. I had told you, he is a womanizer. He tries to take every woman who is willing right to his bed. Well, he also has a drinking problem, and he was arrested a few times for being belligerent in the bar when I worked in Monaco. I saw him in the casinos any time I went near there. He was constantly at the blackjack tables. I heard he is thousands of dollars in debt. He will be at Durand forever. He asked Egidio for early paychecks several times. He has a serious gambling problem. All said and done, I still feel he does a terrific job here at Durand." Antonio said.

"Antonio, I don't plan to live or go on vacation with Andre, so I feel like this. This will not happen again. You have a cell phone to call and say you would be late. You deal with Andre, but I repeat, this will not happen again." Ann said.

"I hear you loud and clear and I agree, this will not happen again. I respect and love you."

Antonio realized he crossed a line. He went to the guest room to sleep that night.

Chapter 6

ANDRE CROSSES THE LINE

There were three yachts going out this week alone. I really was feeling overwhelmed. Antonio was as much help as what he could be, however the changing of themes to accommodate the clients who booked was unreal. I never thought people could be so self-serving until Egidio and I took over Durand. It is a quite different life than the way I was brought up by my parents and grandmother.

Now it is my business to please those clients that rarely can be satisfied. They seem to love control and have everyone at their beckoned call, because they can. Most of the time their requests are to see if we, the yacht company can perform or provide. It appears to be a sick game with them.

I went down to the marina office to talk with Andre to make sure he had everything on his end under control. He was the only one in the office. I opened his office door and he asked me to sit down next to his desk. He got up from behind his desk, came around and grabbed me to kiss me. He was holding tight. I pulled away and we both landed on the floor. He proceeded to hold me down, pull my panties down and insert himself into me. I screamed, but no one heard me. I got up, ran out and could not get my composure. I could not possibly tell Antonio and ruin his trip. I threw up outside, I was so nauseated. I stopped at the nearby coffee shop to get a grip and try to come down before I went home. Now what? We desperately need Andre to run the company, but how can I ever deal with him going forward.

I arrived home and immediately took a shower and changed clothes. I told Collette I would be taking a nap in my room and to take messages if anyone called. The past moments kept running through my mind. I was crying in my pillow. I then thought I better get my face together before Antonio came home.

Antonio came home and asked Collette where I was. He came to my room. I was in the bathroom, putting makeup on.

"What's the matter Ann? Are you not glad to greet me, a little kiss or hug?"

"Oh, Antonio, I am tired, getting three yachts out this week. Here's a big hug. Let's go to the living room and have some tea."

"Wouldn't you want a glass of wine, Ann?"

"Not just now. Thanks though."

"Ann, you know how much I love you. You are the best thing that has ever happened to me. I am here for you if there is anything you want to share."

"Antonio, you are special to me. Thanks. And how was your day? The time is getting close. I am excited for you."

"Seems everything is going as planned. Cannot wait to snorkel and do some diving, maybe even a bit of fishing off the boat." Antonio said.

We went to bed early that night, kissed good night and fell asleep. I was restless all night. I couldn't get the incident off my mind and had no one to tell about it.

Chapter 7

LAURA VISITS

The dates were set for Antonio's trip. He would be leaving June fifth. I called Laura, my long-time friend to catch up on what was going on in her world. She, since I had seen her, got married to a neat guy named Robert. He owned a financial company in New Haven, Connecticut. He was on the road a lot as there were several offices in different states. They had no children as Robert was sterile. Children were not on Laura's list so that worked itself out. She had planned on a trip on the second week in June as Robert was going to a convention. That was perfect for me. She agreed we would go on a one-day ferry to Monaco and go boutique browsing. Antonio knew the hotel owner.

We would split the ferry trip into 2 days. We would stay at Hotel Hermitage.

Andre was beside himself when I told him that I would be gone at the same time Antonio would be on his trip. I texted him as I could not stand the sight of him. We had enough staff to run the company for a year already. Caroline was extremely efficient in the office, setting up dates with clients. Julien was with Durand when Egidio's father was still alive. Everything was well managed by Julien. Claud seemed nervous lately. He didn't talk much. I thought he might have personal issues, but he never as long as I knew him shared anything personal.

Antonio and Alessandro were seeing each other every day in preparation for a wonderful experience. They were sailing in good weather. Each Antonio and Alessandro were experienced sailors. Claud would go with them as he knew all the mechanics of any boat, including all our yachts. If anything would go wrong, Claud is the man.

Only two days before the trip, Alessandro's mother had a serious fall and as Alessandro was an only child, he had to be with her and could not go on the trip. Antonio and Claud always got along, all said and done, Antonio made the decision to go on the trip. Claud didn't say much when he heard Alessandro wasn't going. He was such a private man no one could get inside his mind.

June fifth came quick. Antonio was anxious. He had wanted to go snorkeling in Calavos. It is located between Corsica and Sardinia. He wanted a quiet and serene spot. It is an exotic hideaway. It is almost impossible to find it on a map.

I had only a few days to plan. I was in charge to see that the clients had everything they demanded, to be able to relax when Laura arrived. There is no room for mistakes at Durand. We charge, they pay, and they will get what they want either monetarily or a drop of your blood.

Antonio and Claud sailed. Seemed everything went well for takeoff. I was working on paperwork and making sure Ms. Balencia had all her needs met. She was our highest paying client.

Pierre, my driver picked Laura up at the airport. She arrived rather late. The flight had an issue, and the flight was delayed. Pierre had to wait a couple of hours until she arrived. It was near lunchtime when Laura arrived.

I heard the van door and ran out of the house to meet them.

"Laura, it's been so long." We hugged, kissed on each cheek and the tears flowed, happy tears.

"Laura, you look wonderful. How are you? Your hair is really long and blonde. I must stop gushing so you can breathe. Let's go in."

"Ann, this place looks like a plantation. It is breath-taking. I am thrilled to be here and see you. Wow, what a long trip. May I throw my shoes off?"

"Oh, for God's sake, yes Laura. You know me. Make yourself at home. Don't be intimidated by my new life. I have not changed; I am still the hometown girl from Connecticut. You want some tea or maybe something stronger?"

"I need to sit, put my feet up and relax. I will have a glass of water."

"I have lavender water, okay?" Ann remarked.

"Don't really know what that is, but sure."

"Collette gathers the lavender flowers. She cooks the dried flowers with the water and then lets it cool. She puts it through a strainer. We serve it over ice cubes. She makes a batch every three days. It tastes better fresh." Ann explained.

"Let's go down near the water, at the gazebo. I already had Colette make us a few chicken croissants for lunch. I want to hear all about Robert and when did this happen? I had been busy last year with the Egidio situation. I know you heard about that. It was interna-tional news because of Durand. I didn't think I could make it through his death. Let's go down to the water and relax. Colette will bring us some water and snacks." Ann suggested.

We sat down at the table and chairs in the gazebo. Laura began her story.

"I met Robert when I stopped in his office building to meet with a new accountant. Robert was walking the opposite way in the hall, and I dropped my armful of folders right in front of him. The papers scattered right in his pathway, blew all over the floor and almost tripped him. We both bent down to pick up the papers and our eyes caught." Laura said.

"Ohhhh, your eyes are radiant." Robert said.

"I blushed and then he reached out his hand to get me up from the floor. I had no idea who he was and then the accountant I was going to see came out of his office."

"Oh, Mr. Connor. I did not know you were in town." He said.

"He left and went on down the hall. I went into my accountant's office. George has been doing my accounting for my counseling business for quite some time." Laura continued.

"Do you know Mr. Connor?" George, my accountant asked.

"No, I never saw him before."

"I can't believe you never heard of him. He owns this building and half of New Haven. Going forward, you will see his name all over."

"We took care of our business and I left. The next day, my accountant George called me."

"Laura, Mr. Connor wanted your phone number and I told him I would have to get your permission."

"Yes, but I don't know what he wants though."

Next day "Mr. Connor" called.

"Laura, this is Robert Connor. We met yesterday in the hall. I don't mean to be too forward, but I would enjoy if you would join me for lunch at Claire's Corner Copia."

"I was nervous, but I went, and the rest is history. Every minute is a real joy. We still cannot get enough of each other. Whatever I want, he wants. I feel like I died and went to heaven. Enough about me, I made the short story long as I often do. Now I want to hear about you." Laura said.

"Here comes Colette with our lunch. I'll catch you up afterward."

Colette brought us croissants on a bed of lettuce, chicken salad with thin slices of cantaloupe. Strawberry slices arranged on the side. We already had our lavender water.

"Laura, I have to say, I miss Egidio as he was extremely attentive and loved me deeply. Now Antonio is a different person. He is always there for me to help with Durand as well as being my best support personally. Now Antonio is fantastic in bed. He knows every little thing that makes my heart throb. Maybe that's a bit TMI, but I never knew a man to be such a great lover.

Now Laura you might want to take a short nap, due to the time change. I have done that trip a couple of times; I know how wearing it is. I will make reservations for tonight. I will go to see how Andre is handling things at the marina.

Laura, before you go for your nap, I really need to share something that I could only ask your advice about."

"Ann, you look about to cry. Come here and let me hold you while you tell me. You know I love you as a sister and am here for you."

"Laura, one morning, a couple of weeks ago, I went into the office. Andre, the manager was there alone. I sat at his desk; he got up from the desk, looked at me strangely came around to where I was sitting, and grabbed me and kissed me. As I fought him, we both landed on the floor, and he raped me. I cannot tell Antonio for a couple of reasons. One, I don't want to ruin his trip and secondly, we need Andre at our company. He is the best in the yacht industry to handle the yachts and deal with our clients. I have to go see him now and make sure everything is set so you and I can go to Monte Carlo."

"Oh my gosh, I can't believe he had the nerve to attack his boss. I am so sorry you had to deal with this. I am glad I came here at this time to support you. Do you want me to go with you to the office?" Laura asked.

"No, Laura, but thanks for letting me vent. I could tell this to only you. I will be alright. I will talk right to the point at the door of his office and leave. Caroline is in the office today; I will be safe."

I walked Laura to her room, put a light cover over her and left for the marina.

I came into the outer office, and I heard Andre was screaming at the phone with someone and then he said, "Alright, you got it done. Are you sure?"

I stayed near the door of the outer office; I wasn't going in any further. I asked was there a problem. He said, "It was one of the guys working on a yacht."

"Is there something we need to do?" Ann asked.

"Na, I got it under control." He said that everything was going okay. I left immediately after checking with Andre and returned home.

Laura was still asleep in her room. Pierre had taken her luggage up earlier. I called La Merenda for dinner at seven.

Laura came down and was still yawning. I told her I remembered those trips and how fatigued she must be.

"Have a cup of tea, Laura. That will bring you back to life. Tomorrow we will leave early on the cruise. It's a day cruise to Monte Carlo. We will take a ferry and you will see the glitz and glamour of Monaco. The cruise goes along the French Riviera, and we will stop and see the yachts and shop in the elite shops of Monte Carlo. Maybe we will leave some cash in the casino."

Pierre was at the door exactly at six to take us to La Merenda. I thought we could drink a little more if Pierre would take us back and forth. As we arrived at the restaurant, we were met at the door and given the best table with a scenic view. Antonio knew every chef in Nice. We were always treated special. This place is quaint and only has a small number of tables. It is an intimate dining experience with great food.

Laura was astonished at my new lifestyle. She looked around the restaurant in amazement. The ambiance was charming.

"Laura let's go back to my place, go down to the gazebo and have a glass of Frangelico.

I hope Antonio and Claud are having as good a time as we are. He was wanting to go on this trip sailing for a long time and then when I needed him to help me after Egidio was gone, he postponed that trip."

We talked till the early hours to catch up with the gang back home. Morning came swiftly. Pierre took us to meet the boat. Laura couldn't believe my new life and all of everything.

"I can't believe you are the same girl I knew in New Haven. It's like you are on a second life," Laura said. We took the cruise over to Monte Carlo. When we got off, we strolled along the waterfront and then we went into this specialty boutique, Monte Carlo Forever. Five gold veined marble steps in and then a black wrought iron fillagree railing up to second floor with veined gold marble stairs. Laura bought a great red leather purse with a gold medallion closure. I did not need one more thing as Antonio and I had been here before. We did stop in the casino and Laura won $500. She could not believe it. I called it beginner's luck. We ate lunch at Horizon Rooftop and had a quick sandwich there. We went to the hotel and had dinner. We stopped in every boutique we could before we had to get back to the boat. We arrived back home the next evening at about midnight. Each of us went to our rooms and fell to sleep immediately.

Chapter 8

WHAT IS A BITCOIN?

*I*t was about 10:30 the next morning and a knock came on the front door. It sounded like a desperate knock. I ran to the door with my robe on and opened the door to see Andre. I was frightened because of the past situation. Laura was a late sleeper and was still sleeping. I hated seeing Andre, but we needed him right now at least until Antonio came back or until I could replace him.

"Ann, Ann, Caroline, in the office, brought this letter to me and said this is marked special delivery for Mrs. Durand and to please see she gets it immediately. Caroline said that she never met this man before he delivered it." Andre said.

I tore open the letter and practically passed out cold. It read: Mrs. Durand, if you want to see your friend, Antonio again, you will need to comply with the demand for $800 thousand dollars to be delivered to Bitcoin account #7769 by midnight June 12. The failure to comply will result in his demise.

"Andre, Is this for real or a hoax? I handed him the letter to read. I don't understand bitcoins. Now that I think about it, Antonio was calling every day and he hasn't called for 2 days. I figured he was just having such a good time. It sounds like it is real, but what could have happened, Andre?"

"I have a hard time believing this. Antonio and Claud are both capable sailors and who knows about their trip, and who knows you have money to pay the ransom? The question is why? I will support you in any way I can. I can help you with the bitcoin thing if you decide it is the best solution to pay."

"Andre what can I do? You know how I feel about you, but right now I need your help. Should I get the police involved or maybe that would put them in more danger. Who would want to hurt Antonio or Claud? Antonio is well liked by everyone he knows. That seems to be an odd amount to be asking for." Ann replied.

"Ann, you do realize it is well-known you are the President of Durand and have plenty of money and it also well-known you really love Antonio, and that you would do anything to ensure his safety. There could be any number of suspects. You must decide for yourself. I don't want to be responsible for giving you a wrong decision. I personally think involving authorities could put Antonio in danger. I must get back to the marina because without Claud, it has been rough for me." Andre stated. He left angered.

Laura came down, yawning. "I heard a man's voice. Who was here?"

"Laura, I am beside myself. My heart is beating out of my chest. It was Andre with a letter marked Special Delivery. Read this. I am scared and sick to my stomach. What should I do?"

"Who would do this to Antonio and where is Claud?" Laura queried.

"Good question." Ann replied.

"Now Andre really was no help. I have no idea what to do. Maybe I should call Mom, however I don't want to worry her. Furthermore, she probably would be of no help. I need to breathe, settle down and figure this out." Ann lamented.

"First Ann, do you have that much disposable money? Second, what assurance would you have that Antonio would be returned. We don't even know where they are at this point." Laura said.

"Laura, I am frightened, what would my life be worth without Antonio. I lost Egidio and Antonio has always been there for me, and I so love him. I couldn't go on. I don't have the strength to live my life alone."

42

"Ann, I am here for you and the world still needs you. Let us look at the options. First you need to have some breakfast so you can think. I will get Collette to at least get you a baguette or something. I know you don't feel like eating right now, but you must."

"I haven't heard from Antonio for three days. That makes this deal sound very possible. He has his cell and probably Claud does also. Money really is no issue. Hopefully, money is the only issue for these guys. Thursday is June 12. I must make the decision tomorrow. I can go to my financial advisor and ask him about bitcoin."

After breakfast, I knew better, but decided to call Mom.

"Mom this is Ann. I don't want to alarm you, but I need your input. I am scared and worried."

"Stop Ann, I can hardly understand what you are saying. You are speaking so fast, and you sound breathless. Now start over. I am here for you."

"Mom, Antonio is on a sailing trip, and I got a letter that he is being held for ransom. I don't know what to do. I cannot get him on his cell. It appears dead."

"Ann, I don't know what to say. I wish I could advise you. I would hope if you did pay the money, they would release him because they just wanted the money."

"Mom, I will try to figure this out. I need to decide by tomorrow. I will call you with more information when I decide. Bye I love you."

"Laura it's just you and me and I am counting on you to help me make the best decision. I have to do some decorating for the yacht that is going out tomorrow. This client is impossible and keeps changing his mind. It is a gay event, and he wants all DVD's to be pornographic, men's magazines on every flat surface, and condoms in every drawer and the crew have to be only studs."

"Oh, Ann what a job you have. I could never do what you do. It seems like constant stress. Ann, the decision for the ransom will have to be made with a list of your options, if you do not want to involve law enforcement. Let's us get a cup of tea, have some lunch, sit down and write down your options." Laura suggested.

"Agreed." said Ann.

Colette brought us a salad and 2 glasses and the bottle of Prairie Fume. She brought a plate of macaroons too.

"Laura, whatever I do it has to be soon. First, I can pay the ransom and pray that's all they want is the money and will release Antonio. Second, I will have to get authorities involved and worry if I am putting Antonio in harm's way. Either way, I am scared. I cannot understand what is happening. Who knew where Antonio and Claud were going or where they are at? Who would want to harm them? That makes me think it would be money they want. I am going to my financial advisor today to see how to get bitcoins sent out. I hope he knows how to accomplish that, and I need to insist this is totally confidential to keep Antonio safe, and then how to get it to them on time. Laura, I am sorry to have to go out today, but hopefully you can enjoy the pool and relax until I come back."

Chapter 9

ANN MEETS WITH MR. LAVIGNE

*C*alled our financial advisor and set an appointment for later today. I told him this was an emergency, and we did have priorities with him due to the amount of our money he held.

One o'clock, I had my appointment. Mr. Lavigne came out and greeted me and saw the scared look on my face. I explained the situation and my desperation to free Antonio.

"You can count on me Mrs. Durand. Your confidence is of utmost importance to me."

"Well Mr. Lavigne, I need $800,000 in bitcoin to go to a certain account immediately. I know nothing about bitcoins, and I need to get them to this person's account now."

We discussed all the facts and Mr. Lavigne said to me, "There is some, just some good news. I guess Egidio took care of all your transactions for Durand and your personal finances. What you evidently don't know, Egidio had a bitcoin account set up and there would be enough in the acct to pay the ransom. When he died, we had all accounts set up in your name and that is one of them. I would not suggest paying the ransom. I would suggest getting authorities involved. However, you are my client, one of my best and I cannot tell you what to do." Mr. Lavigne stated.

"Thank God I have you to tend to my affairs. I want to go ahead, and you do what you need to, to accomplish the transaction. The bitcoin account I need to send to is #7769. I want to do it today." Ann said.

"I plan not to advise you on this transaction, I want you to understand, I will do it on your say so." Mr. Lavigne stated.

"Thank you for your assistance. You may have saved Antonio's life."

"I will tell you, just so you understand, this transaction will immediately go into that other account, all in one day and it cannot be stopped once you do it. Are you understanding this, and do you still want to go forward, Ann?"

"Yes, for sure. I have no other option."

I arrived home at dinner time and Collette had made Ratatouille Tart. Laura said she always enjoyed eggplant, and this would be a real treat.

The following morning, Laura had to leave. "Ann, I can hardly bare to leave you with this burden, but Robert and I are going on vacation on the weekend. I need to take care of my man and you. I will be as near as your cell. Just call me, day or night." Laura said.

Pierre took Laura to the airport.

I called Mr. Lavigne to see if the transaction had gone through, he said it had.

I called my doctor to see if he would prescribe something to calm me down, but because I could not tell him of a reason for him to give me something, he suggested an appointment. I said that I would call him back. I could not tell him my dilemma.

I tried to lay down, but sleep did not come. I went out for a run. I only ran a mile, thinking that might help. No such luck. I couldn't call Andre, the way I felt about him. Couldn't call Antonio or Claud. I had to take deep breaths and get through this thing. I took a couple sleeping pills left from Egidio yet and finally dozed off. The next day that crazy client had more requests for a special case of champagne. Not just any champagne, but Veuve Clicquot Yellow label Brut Champagne. Because it is $360 a bottle, the stock anywhere is limited. They wanted several cases. The champagne was not the issue, the number of bottles and the availability were. I worked on getting that all morning, getting it on time that is.

In the afternoon, the phone rang. I ran to get it. Nowadays I would never know who would be calling.

Chapter 10

THE SURPRISE PHONE CALL

"Ann, Ann it is Antonio. I am so glad to hear your voice. I don't know what happened, but our cell phones went dead for quite a while. I seemed to have brain fade for a while, the air seemed heavy. Claud's cell was dead too. We are having a great time and the scenery is fabulous. I did some diving. We did some fishing, and I caught some big fish. and I cooked to entertain ourselves and try to figure out what the problems might be."

"Antonio, you do not realize what happened here!! I am thankful you are alright. I thought I would never see you again. I was sent a letter saying you were being held for ransom."

"WHAT? I can't believe I heard you right. Say that again. We are fine. Nothing happened here. We lost power on our cell phones, and I was feeling rather dizzy for a few days here. I guess the heavy air, the humidity was causing me to feel kind of out of it." Antonio said.

"Antonio, you must be kidding me! They insisted I pay the money by last Thursday or you would be dead. I had no way without calling authorities to try to save you."

"Ann, Claud and I are turning around and coming to you, and we need to get to the bottom of this. Sweetheart I want to be with you. I am so very sorry you went through this. How much money did they ask for?" Antonio asked.

"I hesitate to tell you, since you are safe. We will talk when you arrive home safely."

"Ann, if I could fly, I'd be there sooner. We will be there in two days. I need to be with you and find out exactly who did this despicable thing. I love you. Do nothing until I get there, and we WILL get to the bottom of this."

"Antonio, all that matters now is you are safe. I can't picture my life without you, stay safe and I can't wait to see you and to hold you. Laura had to go home to go on vacation with Robert."

"I need to tell Claud and see what he thinks happened. Hang tight until I get there." Antonio said.

"This is a real huge disaster. I paid the money to whom, for what. This really needs a deep investigation. I love you, bye Darlin'." Ann said.

I need to relax until Antonio gets back and we can work on a resolution. I had shared with Collette our current situation and ongoings.

"Colette made Manicotti for dinner tonight. I enjoy her recipe. Her mother is Italian, and she uses her mom's recipe, I think you and I, Collette will eat at the Gazebo tonight. We can invite Pierre also. It's a beautiful night and I want you to enjoy yourself and I need you here. "Ann said.

"Ann, I know it's not for me to say but, I think we should at least try to find out who would want to hurt you and Antonio or who is against Durand. Who that you two know needs money so bad they would hurt you?" Collette asked.

"If I only knew those answers, I don't. Please let you and I keep this to ourselves, Collette."

We later invited Pierre to join us this night. I noticed Pierre didn't eat much. Maybe he was uncomfortable because usually, Collette and he ate in the kitchen. We all needed to bond. Pierre did not know the big issue. I thought by inviting him we would not talk about the dilemma and have a peaceful dinner.

Well, the day had come and gone for Laura to fly back to New Haven and her honey and for Antonio and Claud to return.

Pierre was under the weather, so I drove down to the Marina. Antonio just texted that they would be docking within the hour.

The hour passed slowly and then I saw the boat coming in. Antonio came off first.

"Darlin', I am so glad you are safe. I want to hold you 'til morning. I will not let you go."

"Ann, I am so glad to be home with you and it is bittersweet. I feel awful what you must have gone through. We must figure this all out and get to the bottom of this horrific situation. I hope we can recover your money too. I love you so very much and cannot live with the guilt I feel for putting you through this."

"Where did Claud go? He left so quickly." Ann asked.

"I think the whole trip was overwhelming to him. He probably wanted to get home."

We were both anxious to get back home. I drove, usually Pierre drove, but I wanted these moments to be private and he was not well.

Colette made Lasagna for dinner because it is Antonio's favorite. Egidio had that for his favorite too. A small tear needed to be wiped from my eye as I thought of Egidio.

Chapter 11

PIERRE IS NOT FEELING WELL

*C*olette said that Pierre wasn't feeling well yesterday and today he stayed in bed. It is very unusual for him. He has always been extremely well; however, he is getting up there. He has seemed to be with the family forever as our gardener, chauffer and friend.

After dinner I felt like I should knock on Pierre's door. He did not answer. I opened the door and he looked pale and was shivering. I called to Antonio.

"Antonio come in here. Do you think we should call Dr. James?" Ann asked.

"Pierre, Pierre, how are you feeling?" Antonio asked.

Pierre just looked up and said nothing.

"Ann, call Dr. James right now." Antonio insisted.

I got a warm blanket to put over him and called. Dr. James knew Pierre, said he would be able to come out in an hour. The hour never seemed to pass. Antonio and I had our own things to figure out. It is too much at one time. I got sick to my stomach lately.

Colette went to the door and let Dr. James in to see Pierre. He checked him out and decided Pierre should be taken to the hospital for a better verdict.

Antonio was so exhausted but stepped up to drive. He and I took Pierre to Hospital Pasteur where Dr. James practiced. We checked him in and would have to wait for some tests the doctor suggested.

We drove back home and didn't speak much. So much was happening, all at one time.

It was late; we mainly just held each other. I couldn't help tearing up as I tried to be strong during this event and now, I had my Antonio back, no matter the exorbitant amount of cash lost. We fell asleep in each other's arms.

It was ten in the morning and Dr. James called. "Please, Ann, come into my office at 1 this afternoon to talk about Pierre." I agreed and he was there promptly. Dr. James said that Pierre had given him permission to tell us that he was terminal. Pierre was always private; one never knew his thoughts. Pierre had been doctoring for the last four months and knew he was dying of liver cancer. The doctor said his demise would probably be within the week. I went into Pierre's room to see him.

He said," Ann, the Durand's were my only real family. My parents died in a car accident, when my father had a seizure behind the wheel and the car went off into a ravine. I was a young boy and my aunt raised me. She really didn't want me, but she was the only relative to take me. She never wanted children and had none of her own. I was only an interruption of her social life. I came to work at Durand as a young man and Egidio's mother, Marianna took me under her wing. I have had a good life here at Durand and am ready to leave this earth knowing Egidio's parents loved me as their own."

"Egidio loved you and I love you too, Pierre." I said as tears streamed down my face.

I held my head down, not to show Pierre my distress. I hugged him and told him that I would be back tomorrow.

That night the phone rang. Antonio went to answer, and it was the hospital. They asked who he was, and he answered that he was a family friend.

They told him not to tell me until, the clergy came over that Pierre passed.

"Who was that? Ann asked.

"I don't know what they wanted."

Within the hour there was a knock at the door and Collette ran to the door. We weren't expecting anyone.

"Ms. Ann Durand, please."

He identified himself from the church nearby.

I came wondering who was there.

"Mrs. Durand, I am sorry to hear of your loss."

"No, no, Antonio, that was mean of you not to tell me. You should have told me; you should have told me," as I was beating on his chest.

Antonio felt dumbfounded as they told him not to say anything ahead. Guess the clergy thought I already knew.

God, how much can a woman take, I thought. Antonio tried to hold me, but at this moment I was angry that all this was happening to me and all at once. Maybe I should have never moved to France. Antonio had to call the doctor and get a prescription. I could not deal with all this alone.

"Ann, take this pill and go lay down in your bed and try to get some rest." Antonio suggested.

Antonio wanted to get the whole story of the ransom deal, but he realized this was going to have to wait. He still couldn't figure what really happened.

I slept about an hour. I was drained. I decided to get up. Antonio came to our room.

"Collette, will bring some tea for you Ann. Sweetheart, I just want to love you and take care of you in any way I can." Antonio said.

Chapter 12

UNCOVERING THE MYSTERY

"I feel better, and we really need to talk about what I thought was a kidnapping and who would do such a thing. First, I need to make arrangements for a cremation for Pierre. We don't need to have a service as we are his only family. I will use the same mortuary as we did for Egidio. I can't believe I would ever have to go through this yet one more time."

"As far as I was concerned it was only that Claud couldn't figure out why we had no power to our cells. The boat had no issues, but our cellphones were both dead. It was about three days, Claud worked to figure out what was wrong with the cell service. We fished and I cooked them and we enjoyed the scenery and then Claud noticed that his phone was working, and I should see if I had power. I did and that's when I called you immediately." Antonio said.

"Let's go out to La Cucina for a bite now and continue this discussion tomorrow." Ann begged.

It was late when we came home, but Antonio wanted to hold me and caress me. I had a lot on my mind however Antonio was so charming and was always romantic in bed, it was easy to enjoy his advances.

Morning came soon and reality set in. Colette had baked croissants and the aroma filled the room. We had croissants, tea and jam for breakfast.

"Ann, I know it's early, but I have a suggestion. When I was the chef at Louis VX in Monaco, the owner had a ransom request and he worked it out with this private investigator. I suggest we go and talk with him. I know he is discreet and has worked privately with several unusual situations. He would get it that you want to keep authorities out of the picture."

"Antonio, I would have a hard time trusting someone. I know I trust that you are comfortable with the idea. I will go to see him, if you come with me." Ann said.

Chapter 13

MONTE CARLO GETAWAY

"I will set an appointment when he is available. I must get his name from Giorgio at the restaurant in Monaco." Antonio said.

"Once we get the guy on the case, let's go for a few days to Monte Carlo. I really want full time to spend with you and relax." Ann suggested.

Antonio called Giorgio and got the name of the investigator, Mr. James Garnier. He told us he wanted to interview all the major employees at Durand. We told him we would be out of town for several days and he was welcome to call us as it was just a getaway.

We decided to stay at Louis XV as we enjoyed it before, and Antonio and I knew several of the wait staff and the chef there. We left on Tuesday and told Andre to be in charge and call us if he needed. He had full staff now as Claud was back, and vacations were over. We planned to come back on Saturday.

We decided to drive in order to enjoy the coast. Chef Germain met us in the restaurant. He had upgraded our room to the main suite. We had a sofa, loveseat with floral prints. The chairs were striped. A dining set was also in the suite. He invited us to sit at the Chef's table this evening. Antonio and he hugged and were glad to see each other. He greeted me also. We went up to the room and the luggage was already there. Antonio threw me on the bed and ravished me. He threw the covers back, undressed me and kissed me all over my body.

"Sweetheart, I couldn't wait to come off the boat and back to you. I missed you so much. Your body is smooth and gorgeous."

We made love and dozed off for a couple of hours and it was time to shower and dress for dinner.

"Ann, you look dynamite in that color."

My dress was fitted, short and red with red strappy shoes. Antonio wore a black and white striped shirt with a black jacket. He sure makes me hot. His shirt was open at the neck and his dark hair peeked out.

We met Germain and his girl Celine. The Chef had created Chateau Briand. He brought out a bottle of Lafite Rothchild from his wine cellar. Crème Brule was the dessert.

It was late when we got back to the room, but it didn't take much persuasion from Antonio to get into love making.

Next day we sat around the pool, swam a bit and caught up on some reading.

The time went quickly and Saturday there were already two yachts needing to be furnished and ready to go in one week when we got back.

Monday Antonio went to the city to pick up items for the sailboat and have lunch with Alessandro and see how he was doing with his mother. When Antonio came home it was near dinner.

"You won't believe who I ran into today at the restaurant. Remember Juliette, when we went on the trip with you and Egidio. She was walking by as we sat outside. She has a little girl now. We didn't talk, she just passed by. I don't think she noticed us."

"Oh, I remember her when the four of us went to Hawaii. She and I got along well on the trip. We sat together on the plane. Did you and Alessandro have a nice visit?"

"Yeah, we did, and his mother is coming along pretty good."

Chapter 14

MR. GARNIER STARTS
TO INTERVIEW

*N*ext morning the phone rang, and it was Mr. Garnier.

"I need to talk with several employees at Durand for openers. Will you please make a time when I can come to Durand and interview them. As we have talked, I would like to begin with Andre, Claud, Antonio, Caroline and Julien. After that I will compile my notes and we can continue to uncover more information to get to the bottom of this. I have confidence I will come through for you."

I decided to have them there on Thursday. Julien was out that day.

Andre was the first to be interviewed. All said and done, no new information was uncovered. Andre was defensive, saying he had enough to do to keep Durand going without Claud being at the marina.

Claud was interviewed next. Claud seemed nervous as he always was. He had something in his background that we will never know. Claud said, "I found my cell phone was dead and I asked Antonio to try his. He had no reception either. After a couple of days trying, I succeeded and was able to get a dial tone. I asked Antonio to try his phone and he was able to get ahold of Ann. We had been so far out on the water that we couldn't contact anyone. We knew nothing of the ransom until we arrived home."

Caroline was interviewed next. She said, "A man came in the door of my office and said that there was a special delivery letter for Mrs. Durand. I thought he probably was from FedEx or some other company. I paged Andre to come to the office. He agreed to run up to the Durand home and deliver the letter to Ann. I had never seen this man before nor since so I don't have any more information. I've told you everything I know."

Mr. Garnier called me at home. "Ann, Julien is not here, and I have another client to see yet today so I will get back to you as soon as I can and going forward you may call me James, please."

"Antonio, I want to go to Les Amoureux tonight. They have the most unusual pizzas. How about it? I am hungry for a pizza. They have the one I like, swordfish cream pizza, fiordilatte mozzarella, hand cut olives and sundried tomatoes." Ann said.

"You know Ann, famous minds travel the same tracks. My exact sentiment. Hop in the car let's go."

On the way, Antonio was very romantic. "Ann, you are the most beautiful woman in the world. I don't mean to be trite, but you are beautiful inside and out. I love you so much. You make my heart sing. You are the best thing that has ever happened to me. I know I was a bit of a womanizer, but I have never been with a real woman as you are."

"Antonio, you can keep saying those things all night long. I never get tired of hearing them."

We both started to laugh and giggle. I knew the night was going to be good. We got home about 10. Antonio wanted to go right to bed, but I was up for a nightcap. He agreed and we went out to the gazebo near the water, with two glasses of Grand Marnier. It was a starlit night. We both agreed we enjoyed spending time together.

"Okay Ann, time to tuck you in."

We held hands and went up to the house and Antonio headed right for the bedroom. I wasn't far behind. He put on soft music and slid into bed and with his long hairy arm was patting my pillow with his hand. He reached for me and grabbed the hem of my nightie, pulled it over my head and threw it across the room. We ravished each other's bodies as the night waned. With the soft music playing, we fell asleep in each other's arms.

Chapter 15

ACCIDENT OR NOT

The next morning the phone rang. Collette picked it up and I overheard her saying, "No it can't be, it can't be. Are you sure? Do you know it was him? I will get Antonio right away."

I wondered why she gave the phone to Antonio rather than me. I ran to the phone as Antonio listened. The conversation sounded intense. Antonio hung up and sat down on the chair distraught.

"Antonio what on earth is wrong?"

"Ann, I don't know what to say. Claud was in his car, and I guess the engine blew up and he is gone. They could barely identify him."

"Who was that on the phone?" Ann asked.

"It was Andre. The authorities called the office because they could not find anything to identify him, but someone in his neighborhood, where the explosion happened recognized parts of his car that were left and knew where he worked. I need to call Andre right now.

Andre, what happened and what did the police say? Antonio asked.

"They could barely read the license plate number. When they did, they were able to find who the car was registered to, and someone at the scene knew he worked at Durand. The police called and asked if I knew Claud De Pere and where he was. I told them he did work here but did not come in yesterday. He is very reliable and did not call in. I called at his home, but he did not answer." Andre said.

Antonio told me what Andre had said.

"I know he had an older car, but I never heard him say he had any trouble with it. I can barely think about it. I really cared about him because he didn't seem to have any family." Ann said.

I called Andre back myself. He basically repeated what he had told Antonio.

"I feel horrible that happened to him and further, you will need to hire someone to replace him like yesterday. I can't do all his work and mine." Andre griped.

"Andre, I know just the person, but right now I can't deal with any more trauma. Think about Claud for God's sake, Andre. Guess Antonio and I will have some type of memorial. He had no family. I don't know if he had any friends: he was so private. I wonder what happened?" Ann questioned.

The authorities came to see me as owner of Durand where Claud worked to see if I knew if he had any enemies because investigators suspected foul play. I really knew nothing about Claud. He always seemed private if not secretive. Whoever thought my life would become like a cobweb. It became so complicated; I was thankful to have Antonio. He did speak up when needed, but he had an uncanny way of calming me. We are a good team as different things raise our ire.

Chapter 16

JULIEN QUESTIONED

"*B*onjour Mrs. Durand. Is Julien back in the office this week? I would like to interview him. He is the only one left of your employees." Mr. Garnier asked.

"Yes, what day and time would you like to do that?"

"May I call you Ann?"

"Definitely, Mr. Garnier, I know James. I will have him to call you direct. You and he can meet in my office."

Mr. Garnier came into the office Friday, and I met him there. He and Julien met in Claud's office. Julien's office had no door. I thought they would want privacy.

"Julien, I am Mr. Garnier. I would like to ask you some questions about what you might share, if anything about the ransom deal Mrs. Durand is going through."

"I don't know why you are asking me. I work here in the office and work with their books. That's it." Julien said.

"Julien, there might be something you overheard in this office by someone else. Did you ever overhear Andre or Claud talking about anything unusual?"

"I only remember one day, the two of them were cursing at each other about a money issue. Claud screamed, "I need it now. I need to make my payments on time, or they will come for me."

Andre then hollered back," You know I don't have the money transferred yet."

"Evidently they had some transaction going on, but it was none of my business, I just forgot about it." Julien quipped.

"When did that conversation take place?"

"It was last Friday; I remember because I wanted to leave early for the weekend to go on a family trip. They were screaming or I wouldn't have paid attention, but one couldn't ignore them."

"Thanks Julien. You may have been the most help so far. I will get back to you if I need you." Mr. Garnier said.

Chapter 17

INVESTIGATION CONTINUES

The National Police and the Gendarmerie got involved with Claud's death as facts seemed not to line up. The questions were with the scattered parts of the car. It appeared to have been caused by an explosive device. They would investigate. I knew of no enemies of Claud. Could I handle any more complications in my life?

"Antonio, I need to go out to dinner tonight to come down. Let's go to my favorite, La Cucina. I love their duck and I know you really enjoy their Salmon. It's time to try to relax." When we came home, we went down to the water and swam for a bit, and we were laughing so hard. We came out of the water, and he grabbed me and wrapped me in a huge beach towel and led me up the path through the living room with my wet feet and tossed me on our bed. He continued to dry me off and kiss my breasts. We made love and fell sound asleep pleasantly.

In the morning, Collette made wonderful, powdered sugar croissants. I could smell them baking from our room.

"Sweetheart, stay tucked in and I will go down and bring you your breakfast. Tea, croissants and some fruit."

Antonio brought a tray with tea, a croissant and a bowl of strawberries and cream. Antonio insisted on feeding me one strawberry at a time. It made me smile and I loved him even more. He always treats me thoughtfully.

"Ann, I am going to have lunch today with Alessandro at Le Garcons. I have not been there, but he says I will enjoy it. He and his lady dine there often. Meeting him at 1. Maybe we could eat light tonight." "Antonio, you won't believe who called me yesterday, Anthony Balencia. Remember Mrs. Balencia, my very, very demanding rich old hag. Tony is her son and wants to buy Durand. I told him it's not up for sale. It's been in Egidio's family for years. I guess his mother thought then she would be the boss and could go on his yachts anytime she felt for free."

"Well Ann, you knew that family was crazy and a lot of trouble. I'm leaving now to meet Alessandro and I'll be back about four." Antonio said.

Chapter 18

ALESSANDRO GOING TO CAPRI

"Heh, Alessi great to see you, I have never eaten here before," Antonio quipped.

"Antonio, Les Garcons has been here forever. I am surprised you have not eaten here. It's a treasure. I have been busy lately. I think I am going to move to Italy. I don't really need to work anymore. I am going on a trip there to Capri next week and check it out." Alessandro said.

"What are you recommending to order?"

"I suggest Poulet Carmelise." Alessandro said.

"Let's have a glass of wine first and tell me why you picked Capri. By the way you remember last time we lunched, and I saw Juliette go by. I looked her up and we met. She told me she wanted to marry me, when we were going together and I left, she wanted to tell me she was pregnant. When she found out I loved her, but did not want to get married, she decided not to contact me and raise the child herself. She did not want to see me if I didn't want to marry her. She does not want anything from me. She is now with a guy who loves the little girl, and they want to raise her. I really don't know if it's mine as when I broke up with her, she was seeing another guy quickly. I can't imagine how Ann would handle this news. I was single at the time. Ann has met Juliette and liked her."

"Antonio, I don't know if you should maybe say nothing, but knowing you, you would want to be true to Ann and tell her. She loves you. We both know that. You will decide but think it over awhile. Sometimes less said, easy mended. It really is a done deal. Now as far as me going to Capri. You know my family is Italian and I enjoy Italy. Why not? I will let you know when I come back."

"I guess I will have to keep the Juliette thing to myself. No value to bringing it up. Ann has enough on her plate." Antonio said.

Antonio came home about 4:30.

Chapter 19

CLAUD'S APARTMENT

"You must have had a lot to talk about, darlin'. I was meeting with the police trying to figure what happened to Claud's car and what we should do now. He has no relatives. They suggested we go to his apartment, and I went with them. We had to get in by the apartment manager letting us in. When they were finished checking it out, I said we would clean it out. They want this done this week. They have done their search of the place. It's just a matter of cleaning it out. I want to go there tomorrow and have it done. I think we will have no memorial, just a cremation as there is no one to be there. His apartment is a bit of a mess, a bachelor pad for sure." Ann said.

Next day Antonio and I went to the apartment. We hired some guys just to get rid of all the furniture. They came at noon and were very good and fast. As they took the bed apart and proceeded to take the mattress and box spring down, something fell out, evidently it was between the mattress and box spring.

"Antonio, what is that? It is metal and I never saw anything like that."

Antonio was aghast. He went white and was speechless. He just kept shaking his head.

"Oh God, I don't want to believe my eyes. It just can't be."

"Antonio, what on earth is wrong with you. Tell me. Speak up!"

"Ann this is a signal jammer."

"What is it used for?" Ann asked.

"It is illegal and used to block cellphone signals. Something is radically wrong here. No wonder we could not get our cells to work. Once the people got the bitcoins, our cells began to work again. Claud was in on all of this somehow. He couldn't have worked alone. We will have to get authorities involved now." Antonio said.

"I will collect all the paperwork from Claud's desk, his checkbook and other stuff and go through it at home much later. Let's talk to Mr. Garnier first and get his uptake." Ann suggested.

"Call him now and let's get an appointment. This is God-awful, Ann."

He was able to see us in two hours at three o'clock.

"We need to eat something before we go. How about Le Bouchon?" Ann asked.

Neither of us ate much. We were both stressed beyond belief. After lunch we went to the Garnier office. Antonio told James what we know. The signal jammer should be the steppingstone to more information. Who was Claud talking to for directions about timing of cell interruption?

Chapter 20

JULIEN REINTERVIEWED

Mr. Garnier thought we should try to expedite the situation more from a background position so as not to signal the guilty person or persons.

"I want to go back and speak with Julien." Julien was at the office. James called Caroline and asked to speak with Julien. He agreed to be re-interviewed.

"Julien, let me ask you this, when Claud and Andre were having that argument about the money, did Andre or Claud say why Andre was to pay Claud? What was the reason for the transaction?"

"Mr. Garnier, I always try to mind my own business. I do my job, that's it. I need my job to support my family." Julien said.

"It's really important for you to try to remember any details we have not yet discussed. It is very important for Mrs. Durand to try to recover her money from the ransom payment and find who took her money." said Mr. Garnier.

"Well, all I know is that Andre was on the phone often and saying the same things. He was on his cell not the desk phone, walking around his office with the door open. I don't think he realized someone could hear him. He always would say on several occasions, "I will have the money soon. I don't have the damn money now." I do know Andre was always going to the casino in Monte Carlo every weekend. He said that James Bond movies were filmed there. I don't know the name. He would leave the office early on a Friday to go there. Other than that, Claud was always to himself. He was very cautious on what he said. Seemed he had some-thing to hide, but we never knew." Julien said.

"I respect your time, Julien and thank you. You have been extremely helpful."

James decided to take a trip to Monte Carlo and try to find where Andre hung out. The Casino de Monte Carlo was where the bond movies were made so he went there. When he arrived back, he called me.

"Ann, what is Andre's last name?" James asked.

His last name is Blanchet, why do you ask?

"I have some new information and I want to go back to Monte Carlo and find out more about Andre as he spends quite a bit of time in the casinos."

"Okay, keep in touch."

I was busy this week furnishing two yachts with very specific, difficult requests. One request was that each sleeping area be decorated as a brothel. A lot of deep red, chiffon draperies at each bedroom doorway and plenty of sex toys. They were into a little S and M also. Not my style so I had to do some research. They paid extra to have specific requests filled.

Antonio was going to help Alessandro work on his sailboat.

"Alessi, how have you been? Heard you sailed this week. I haven't been out since the incident. I can only stay for a few hours. We are meeting with Mr. Garnier tomorrow and I need to help Ann with some work at the marina. I still don't know if I should tell Ann about the Juliette story."

"Antonio, it's the last time I am going to say it. Let sleeping dogs lie. You don't even know if the girl is yours. Maybe that's why she didn't pursue it. You love Ann. She has enough going on right now. All that is in the past. Shut your mouth. Now help me out with this mast."

"You are right buddy. No more said."

Chapter 21

MR. GARNIER IN
MONTE CARLO

*N*ext day we met with James. He said that he found new information in Monte Carlo.

"The casino could not give out information, but I met a man at the blackjack table spending a ton of money. He was mostly losing, and I mean a lot. I sat down and asked him if he knew Andre. I got a picture to take along from one of your brochures. He got angry. He starred at me with a mad look."

"Yeah, do I know him. He's the only guy who loses more money than me. He has lost over six hundred thousand dollars over time. I lost thousands too. We had a love, hate relationship at the tables."

"James, do you think Andre was involved in the ransom thing? Ann asked.

"Ann, I can't say much yet. I want to see if I can find out who bought the signal jammer. It's very possible that it was bought online."

A couple of days went by, and I saw this box on the floor. I forgot I put it there when we were cleaning out Claud's place. I wanted to get rid of that stuff, but I thought maybe in some of his old receipts I could find if he sent for the jammer. It took me about three hours just to go through his credit card statements, line by line, but it paid off. Here it was on a statement from three months ago. Raytheon 4G jammer-$255.00. Well, I am not a detective but now I decided to look in his checkbook to see if there was anything in it. He scribbled. I could barely read his writing; however, he did write everything down. Oh my God, last month there was a deposit for $255.00. I wonder if the dots connect.

I called James right away. He was out. I left a message for him to call me.

James called an hour later, and I explained what I thought might be of interest to our case.

"If the deposit was cash, we will never know. If it was a check, we hit pay dirt. I think it is time to get the authorities involved, Ann."

Chapter 22

POLICE BECOME INVOLVED

I called the police station and asked to meet with an officer. They assigned Officer Benet to me. I told him I wanted to bring James with me.

James and I arrived at 10 am sharp. I was upset. I thought I would give up my breakfast.

"Mrs. Durand, I need to hear your story from the beginning." It took me near an hour to tell him all the details. Officer Benet said he would get back to me. James and I went to lunch.

"This sounds like I will have to confer with the officers on Claud's case and add the information about your case. At any rate, we will have to speak with Andre at your company. He seems to be part of the story. I will get back to you, but I must have your permission to deal with the authorities. They will surely call you in to hear your story directly from you again. Do I have your permission?" Mr. Garnier asked.

"I don't feel at this point, I have a choice. For me to get on with my life, I must have this phase complete. I may not recover my money, but I need some closure on this. So, the answer is Yes.! Get on with it." Ann said.

Now I was always looking around feeling unsafe, not knowing who had it in for me.

When I got home, Antonio was making dinner. He made Calzones. He makes the best with his own sauce. Nothing like living with a chef. Collette had the day off. Dinner was wonderful and he served Chianti and his great French bread.

After dinner we went down to the gazebo, had some Grand Marnier and I told Antonio the events of the day.

"Ann, I think we are now going to be able to nail down the entire story. I have my theory, but think we best be still until the authorities and James put the puzzle pieces together."

"Darlin', I think I suspect Andre is somehow involved, but I like you, think mums the word right now until we hear back."

"Let's take a dip right now. No need to get suits. No one is here. Collette is off tonight. Take off your dress and let's skinny dip." Antonio suggested.

"You are the craziest man I know, a good kind of crazy."

We just threw our arms up and splashed each other wildly. I needed a distraction from all my woes. Antonio is always the one to calm me. He is sooo good for me. I am beginning to see that I want him to be with me always."

It took about a week, and I got a call from Officer Benet. He said that their office wanted to interview me about the case. It took about three hours. They asked a lot of questions about Andre. They said that they would need his number and would call him in tomorrow.

When I arrived home, Collette had dinner ready, and Antonio came back from the marina. We were trying to keep Durand going well even with all these complications.

"Ann, I think we should talk about the possibilities that Andre may end up leaving the company and we should start now looking for someone to replace him and now Claud's job is up for replacement too. We need to fly ahead of the plane."

"Antonio, I am exhausted of all of this. I have an idea for our future, but right now I can barely function."

Chapter 23

A NIGHT WITH ALESSANDRO

It had been several days, and we have heard nothing from authorities or Mr. Garnier, so I called Officer Benet. He was out on a call and would return my call.

He called that afternoon and told me to come in about four today. I got there early, and they took me into Officer Benet's office and there were three other officers there.

"Mrs. Durand, we are reasonably sure your employee is our suspect connecting several things to him. We have been checking our sources and are reasonably sure Andre is involved in both incidents. He appears to be involved in the sailboat incident and now we are suspecting the car explosion is also connected. His answers are vague or completely not being able to be corroborated. We will need to call him in once more. We are checking a few more facts. We will again be in contact with you in about a week. That should be enough time for the ends to be tied up." Officer Benet conveyed.

Antonio and I were invited to go to a Sailing event Tuesday evening. I agreed to go to get my mind off my troubles.

Alessandro oversaw the event on his sailboat. The night was balmy, and Antonio knew everyone and introduced me. Everyone had known Egidio and told me how great a man he was. Music and food were fantastic. We had a fun night and laughed and laughed. I didn't know Antonio was so funny. All the women loved his stories. We got home late, but tonight I wanted to make love. I came out of the bathroom with my red lingerie with black lace on the edges. Antonio grabbed me, kissed me and just couldn't get enough of me. I shocked him as he didn't know how provocative I could be. He enjoyed my boldness. We were getting to learn more about each other each day. Seemed we had so much going on since he came here to live, it was difficult to show each other our common spontaneity.

The week was crazy. Three yachts were going out and details were so unusual that it took the entire staff to have tasks to accomplish Mrs. Balencia's two yacht reservations.

Chapter 24

ANDRE'S INCIDENT

ollette called me to the phone. It was Officer Benet. "Mrs. Durand, is someone with you now?"

"Why do you ask that?"

"Mrs. Durand, are you alone?"

"Well, no Antonio is here with me." I was irritated.

"Please put him on the phone."

Antonio appeared to be in shock. He seemed to be on the phone a long time, then he sat down on a chair. I couldn't hear what the officer was saying, but I could tell it was serious. Antonio hung up.

"Antonio, tell me what bad news is left to tell me."

"Ann, it was Officer Benet. Andre, it appears he committed suicide. Let me tell you the story.

Andre had not come to work yesterday. Caroline called him and he did not answer. Caroline called the manager of his apartment and he called police. He did not want to go in alone.

Ann, the officers went to Andre's apartment, and he did not answer. The car was in the drive; they went to see the manager. He said that Andre had come home late last night, and he had not seen him today and he would need to get the police to go into the apartment.

The officers came. The manager opened the door. Andre was lying on the floor, smelled like alcohol, empty bottle on table and an empty pill bottle on the table too. Called an ambulance, but he was gone. There was an envelope lying on the floor. Officer Benet was the one to notice it and pick it up. With gloves on, he opened it and read it. He read it to me.

"Ann, I cannot go on at Durand. I am sorry for any distress that I have caused you. My life now is useless. I cannot take it any longer. I am sorry, believe me. Andre." Antonio repeated.

"Antonio, I can't deal with this business. Durand is too much for us and now with Andre and Claud both being gone, I know the other guys have been with us long enough to take over those two positions, but I have had it." Ann stated.

"I am having lunch with Alessandro this afternoon. I want to hear more about Capri. He went there a couple of weeks ago. He is thinking about moving there in his

retirement. I could never think of not working myself."
Antonio said.

"I need some serious time off right now, but I will
have to keep this business going. I will talk to the fellows we have and move them around to cover what we
need. Today while you are gone to lunch, I am going
to the marina. I think I have figured out chain of com-
mand. They have had their issues in the past with Andre.
He was a hardline man. That was the ying and the yang.
It made our company the best, however it was the way
he spoke down to the fellows that they never liked him.
Hans and Gerard will be my men. They have been with
us forever and get along with each other. Hans was
Andre's back up man as well as Claud. When Andre was
out, Hans ran the place. He will do a great job." Ann said.

"Let's eat out tonight. You have enough going on.
La Voglia has great food and I know Salvatore, the chef
there. I really enjoy their Linguine au Homard. The lobster is always fresh. They have a great Lasagna al Forno.
I will make the reservation." Antonio said.

"Please make the reservation for about eight as I
want to relax when I get back from the marina. They
don't even know Andre is gone yet."

Chapter 25

THE NEW DURAND

I dealt with the new Durand. Hans will be our main man and Gerard will take Claud's job. I got home, threw my shoes off and got some lavender water and went to my room to lie down. The phone rang. Collette picked it up. It evidently was important as she came to my room to have me pick it up. She said it was a Mr. Anthony Balencia.

"Hello, Ann speaking. What is on your mind?"

"I am calling to see if you still want to hang on to Durand. The last time we talked you weren't interested in selling. My mother asked me to check on whether you would consider selling for a price?"

I really was seriously thinking of selling the company after all that has happened. It was not public knowledge

yet about Andre. Claud's story made the news. I thought
I would play coy and wait to hear his offer.

"I might think on it if the price was out of sight."
Ann replied.

"Well, be real. It has to be good for both of us."

"You and I know Durand has the best yachts and
best company on the French Riviera."

"Ann, you know price is not based on your opinion."

"Anthony, just because you are dealing with a woman,
know I can wheel and deal better than the best of them;
don't get smart. I am holding the ace. Your mother wants
this company so she can go free on her fancy dancy
cruises. Good luck, Anthony if you ever own Durand."

Guess I got a little carried away, but I had put up
with Mrs. Balencia for so long with her outrageous
demands that I just let loose.

"Anthony, I have to think on this and will get back
to you by the end of this week, matter of fact, Friday at
one in the afternoon at my office at Durand."

Antonio came home about four.

Antonio came into the room and kissed me on my
neck and grasped my breasts. He was always a "boob
man", maybe because he was fascinated because men
didn't have them. Well, I never minded as it turned me
on to know he was into me. He is always romantic.

"What do you have behind your back, darlin'. You
have that secret look in your eyes. C'mon, tell me, what
are you hiding?" Ann asked.

Out from behind his back, came a huge bouquet of pink roses with ferns.

"Antonio, I love you so much. In the worst of times, you always make me smile. I have a lot on my mind right now."

"I always try to make it better. I heard a way to a woman's heart is with flowers, my love."

"You always know how to distract me and bring a smile to my face and make me realize you deserve a warm and fuzzy night tonight and you will get it."

Chapter 26

ANTHONY MAKES AN OFFER

"Collette told me that Anthony Balencia called. What was on his mind?" Antonio asked.

"Do you remember he called me a while ago. Same thing. He wants to purchase Durand. I am sure his mother would pay the money. He, I heard has been a mama's boy and would not know the first thing about running a business, however money is money."

"Well Ann, what are you thinking? Are you seriously thinking of selling Durand? Antonio asked.

"I am planning on it. I decided today, unless you can come up with a reason not to."

"Alessandro and I talked today. He has made his decision to live in Capri. He said that it has jaw dropping natural beauty, delicious cuisine, my forte and world class shopping. He said that the cafes are busy 'round the clock. Early morning cappuccino sippers and after dinner aperitifs are on the agenda. Many yachts are anchored there. You would feel right at home. I thought we should go there with him one time and see if Italy has any possibilities for us.

From what I can see online my best bet to be a chef at a restaurant there would be Lo Smeraldo. It has an amazing view of the coastline. Seafood is their specialty. Last, I know Aldo is the chef there. I worked with him in Monte Carlo. The place is family owned. They always seem to care more when it has their family's reputation at stake." Antonio said.

"I am meeting with Anthony on Friday. I want to see Mr. Garnier, my financial advisor, before that. I want to check with him and see if he can come up with a price for Durand, so I have something to work with on Friday. I hope he can be there also. I have some thoughts I have been contemplating for a long time. My background is writing, and I have been studying an idea from Denmark. I have been reading up on a Human Library. I might want to have a brick-and-mortar or Online forums. I am still doing research. The idea really fascinates me, and I could do it anywhere." Ann said.

I went to see Mr. Garnier the next morning and he and I came up with 750 million bottom line. He and I thought I should get 800-850 million. I was anxious to get home and tell Antonio. I was starting to get excited.

This could really happen. Durand was going to be history in my life. Yeah.

When I pulled up in the drive, Antonio came running out to meet me.

"How did your meeting go, Ann?" Antonio asked.

"Anthony doesn't yet know that I am thinking to make a deal. I want to hear his numbers first but have my numbers ready."

"Ann, I guess I really did not know how prolific you are." Antonio said.

"I am not blonde, but I am not a "dumb brunette" either. My grandmother taught me many ideas. One of them was, do not play your ace until you have played every other card first. In other words, know when to hold it and when to fold it. She told me that the metaphor works for many situations. The other lesson I learned from her is, always be a cause-and-effect person. How will your decision play out? Always play out the repercussions of your decisions and you will see clearly the right thing to do."

"Seems like you have everything under control, Ann. Hope Friday goes your way." Antonio said.

Friday was here and it was one o'clock and Anthony pulled up in his blue Bugatti.

"Bonjour, Anthony. Come right into my office. Mr. Garnier will be here shortly. James was in the drive. The three of us sat around the office table. The agreement was that James would only speak if I asked him. Anthony and I would run the conversation.

Once we discussed the details, how many yachts? There were 6. The marina office would be included and the land the property was on. Anthony said that he would keep the employees on for the foreseeable future.

Anthony and I bantered for several hours. I don't think he had a clue what it takes to run these super yachts. He never thought what it took to do all the decorating and filling all the obnoxious demands of the clients. He was thinking you were just taking clients out on a boat ride.

"What is your asking price, Ann?"

"No Anthony, you go first. What are you thinking to offer?" Ann asked.

Ann, I did a lot of research, and I will offer, a generous offer as it is, $750 million."

"We might as well get used to the fact, you and I will never have a deal. You can get real because if you did do your homework, you know Durand is worth much more. We might as well go home as you are dreaming if you think I was born yesterday. I got up from the table, pushed in the chair, picked up my briefcase and said, James the meeting is over, you can leave."

Anthony got up. His mouth was wide open. He didn't know what to say. My impression was that he had no clue. I am sure his mother told him to get the company now.

"Anthony, call me when you come to your senses. I will show you the door." Ann said.

I got home and Antonio saw the look on my face and decided not to ask how things went.

"Collette, will you bring a bottle of Grand Marnier to the gazebo. Antonio, let's go down to the water and I will tell you about the so-called meeting."

We walked down and Antonio poured us each a drink. He sat in silence until I spoke.

"Anthony was a joke. He appeared to have little knowledge of what he was all buying, what it takes to run Durand. I may need a second drink to get over him and his ignorance."

A couple of days went by. I didn't know if Anthony would come up on pricing or if he was speculating.

Collette picked up the phone when it rang. She reached out her hand to me, "Mr. Balencia."

"Ann, I would like to meet at your office tomorrow and talk one more time. How about 2 o'clock?"

"Anthony, make it worth my while or just don't bother. I will meet you at 2 tomorrow." Ann said.

"Collette. I need to let you in on what's going on around here right now. I am planning to sell Durand and then if that works out, we will be selling the house. It is only fair you know, so you can plan accordingly."

Next day, the blue Bugatti pulled up at quarter of two. Anthony strutted up to the office. I was there any way for other business.

"Sit down Anthony and let's get started. What is on your mind?"

"Ann, I have our final offer. Take it or leave it. This company takes a lot to keep going and I never have been one to take on much work. My final offer is 800 million. If that is not acceptable, I will leave."

"Anthony, not so fast. I need to clear that with Mr. Garnier and if we decide, you and I will have to meet again, Wednesday to sign paperwork. Let's meet here, in my office at 3 pm. Does that work for you?"

"I will be there when we sign papers over to me. I know you will take this offer."

"Anthony, you are certainly sure of yourself."

Tuesday, I met with James Garnier, and we agreed to sell at 800 million. He would draw up paperwork and make sure Anthony had enough credit to cover the sale. We knew Balencia's had plenty of money but did not know how much debt they had.

Wednesday could not come soon enough. I was anxious to rid myself of Durand.

Three o'clock sharp, Anthony came strolling in, in his confident self. We sat down with Mr. Garnier.

"Anthony we will hesitantly agree to 800 million. In the deal we will make the transition of ownership on October 1. That will give us time to be sure everything is in order and to have you familiar with our people and details of the sale. Are we in agreement with the terms?"

"Ann, I would not want the transfer of the property and Durand until September anyway, so yes we are in agreement."

I arrived home and met Antonio at the waterfront and had a glass of Pouilly Fuisse. We toasted the sale. Now we would have to make new decisions.

Chapter 27

ALESSANDRO IN CAPRI

"Ann, I was over at Alessandro's home today. He has decided on living in Capri and is moving there next month. He and his lady are both Italians and it seemed like a great decision for them. He is inviting us to come stay for a week with them to see if we would like it there."

"I have heard some wonderful stories of some of our clients about that part of Italy. I would like to go once this sale is complete. What we have not talked about is this property. It is worth a chunk of change also. I feel like I am betraying the Durand family in selling it, however there are no other Durand's to keep it going. I certainly do need a night out tonight. This has been some year." Ann said.

"Let's go eat at Jan," Ann suggested.

Antonio and I left for the restaurant in his black Citroen DS convertible. I always liked his car. It was such a smooth ride beside looking sleek. We discussed all our possibilities. We talked about where to live, what we would do each professionally.

I already had the Human Library idea researched. Antonio always was a chef at heart. He already knew a restaurant where the chef from Monte Carlo had transferred to open his own restaurant. His restaurant was instantly popular as it was a French restaurant in Italy. There were few cafés in Capri.

The dinner was outstanding. We were seated in a far dark corner with low lighting and candlelight. The ride home was balmy with the top down. My hair was blowing in the wind. Antonio looked particularly handsome to me tonight. His dark curly hair was all messy in the wind. I couldn't wait to get home and make love. We pulled in the drive, Antonio put the top up and he reached for my hand, opened the front door and threw me into the stuffed chair in the living room.

"You beautiful creature. I want to ravish you right here. I reached for his hand to pull me up and he led me to the bedroom. I had worn my red lacy bra and panties that day and that just turned him on, and he pulled open the covers and patted the bed and invited me to lie down. We made mad passionate love for hours.

We had not been this emotional recently and fell asleep in each other's arms.

"Bonjour, mon amour. Here's your tea and some fruit. You are cute when you open those baby brown eyes in the morning." Antonio sighed.

"You are so lovable, what would I do without you?"

"You will never have to be without me unless you choose."

All week, I was super busy with four yachts going out, each one day apart. Antonio worked at the dock with the fellows making sure everything was in good repair and training the two fellows for their new roles to fill in for the two men we had lost. They knew our number in the office if they had a problem or question.

With James Garnier's capable work, the sale went surprisingly well. We had a month or so now to get all in tip top shape.

Chapter 28

TRIP TO CAPRI

Alessandro and Antonio talked and decided we would fly to Capri next week. Antonio said that Greta his lady friend, and I would get along well. He had met her several times. She had been a university professor when she was in Nice.

"If you like her, I am sure I would too. I am easy to get along with. You can't be dealing with our crazy clients and not learn to get along with most anybody." Ann said.

Thursday, we headed for the airport. We were certain, Hans and Gerard could run Durand well while we were gone. They had been with the company for a long time. Caroline in the office knew our number and how to reach us if they needed information or if they had a problem. Julien ran the financial department and was very efficient.

We flew into Naples and drove to Capri. Alessandro had a gorgeous property on the water. It had an old-world charm, but it was relatively new. It wasn't that large, but beautiful. It had a stone path with a wood railing going down to the water.

We talked to the late hours and slept in late. It was a pleasant evening and the four of us enjoyed each other's company.

Alessandro made reservations at Lo Smeraldo for the next evening. Antonio wanted to see his friend the Chef Aldo, who now owned this restaurant.

In the morning, the four of us went to town down the narrow streets; high end boutiques were all on one street. Outdoor dining and restaurants were along the way. Art everywhere. Colorful buildings of yellow, rust and blue with a lot of filagree and flowers along balconies. Fushia bougainvillea hung from the walls. I already wanted to move here. We went up the stairwell and ate lunch at Pulalli. We girls each had a seafood salad and the guys each had grilled salmon. We sat at the outdoor terrace.

Chapter 29

ALDO MAKES AN OFFER

*I*n the evening we drove to Lo Smeraldo and met Aldo, the owner of the restaurant. He was a pleasant, short man, a little round I would say and balding. Immediately he said, "Antonio, Antonio, you need to come help me in my restaurant. You are the best. I am inviting you to come back tomorrow in the day and I will give you a tour."

He gave us the best table on the upper level, outside on the veranda and the sun was setting. The sky was an array of yellow, orange and hazy blue. Breathtaking I say.

The seafood was amazing. I had a shrimp entrée and Antonio had lobster. Alessandro and Greta were such caring, fun hosts. We already were loving Capri.

Next day Greta suggested we girls go through the many boutiques. She suggested we start at La Parisienne and move along the Via Camerelle. I ended up purchasing a pair of sandals hand stitched in Capri. I bought a bottle of Limoncello, a liqueur made from Capri's lemons. Antonio has a sweet tooth, so I picked up a package of Torta Caprese, a wickedly, rich chocolate and almond delight.

Antonio wanted to meet with Aldo and Alessandro wanted to go along. Aldo met them at the door as it was Monday, and the restaurant was closed. He suggested they start with a glass of Campari. Aldo showed them the beautiful view by the sea.

"Antonio, I am getting too old to run this by myself. I love the restaurant, but I really need assistance. Who better than you Antonio? You, I trust, and your culinary prowess is best bar none and I like you, Antonio. Think on it. You would like living in Capri."

We all four arrived home about the same time. In the evening, Alessandro had made reservations at Terrazza Brunella. The seafood was outstanding and a great selection of pastas. Their signature Almond Cake was a must. It was known as Torta Caprese. Luigi, the owner's son is making the cake these days. It is known across Italy.

We arrived back to Alessandro's quite late. We retired to our room, as our flight was early the next morning.

Friday morning had a quick breakfast and Alessandro drove us to the airport. We had a lot on our mind now. We almost decided, and we well were convinced to move after this great time in Capri. First things first. I needed to make sure all paperwork for the sale of Durand was in order with Mr. Garnier. We would then place the house up for sale with the realtor. We would take an apartment in Capri until we got the lay of the land. Antonio had been discussing the possibilities for a while now.

Saturday morning, we woke up and propped our pillows so we could talk for a bit. Antonio had asked Collette to bring our breakfast up to our room. Both of us were excited at the thought of our new life. I was anxious to get out of this business, not because I didn't like the yachts, but I had had it with the constant extreme demands of the clients. Antonio always enjoyed being a chef and the restaurant business. He was excited as I was.

Later in the day, I met with James Garnier and to my surprise, all the ducks were in a row, and we were able to close the deal. Durand was sold.

Chapter 30

DURAND HOME FOR SALE

ednesday afternoon, I met with the realtor, Muriel. She said, "This is a unique expensive property; it will take a special client. You have six bedrooms and five baths. Your family hasn't used the full house most of the time, but I think, from what I know of my other client, he would have other family members coming in to stay from time to time. He is moving to Nice from the US. His company is starting a plant in Naples. He will be partially reimbursed to relocate. I will be speaking with him, early next week. The asking price should be 7718,729 million. The location on the water and the amount of property has raised the value."

We agreed to meet as soon as she contacted her client or had another one to see the house.

Chapter 31

CALL ABOUT MOM

Antonio told me Laura called from Connecticut. She wanted you to call as soon as you got home. I was concerned, Antonio sounded as though it might be urgent.

"Laura it's Ann. Is there something wrong?"

"Ann, I guess your mom had come to New Haven to visit with Lisa's mom, Julia. You know they had been friends for years and today, your mom had to go to the hospital here. Julia asked me to call you as she said that she couldn't reach you. Your mom is at Yale New Haven hospital."

"I was in meetings and had my phone turned off this morning. I will call right now."

"May I have the room of Marie Anderson please." The room did not answer. I called the nurse's station. They asked who I was, and I told them I am her daughter."

"I will put her nurse on the phone, please wait."

"Yes, I am her daughter. Why can't my mother speak to me?"

"I am about to explain it to you. She had a serious heart attack and we tried to reach you at the only number we had for you. She is sedated now. It would be wise if you could come to see her. Where are you located?" the nurse asked.

"I am in Nice, France. I will catch a flight as soon as I can, but tell me will she be alright?"

"I am not able to say that for sure. We are keeping her in the intensive care unit until she is coherent. You may call the nurses station and we will keep you informed as we know more."

Antonio pulled out a chair as I almost passed out when I heard the news.

"Darlin', I need to catch a flight to be with my mom. It sounds as this is extremely serious."

"Are you flying to New York? Antonio asked.

"No, she was on a trip. She is in New Haven, Connecticut visiting her friend. She is in the hospital."

"Sweetheart, I will take care of everything here. Get a flight reservation and I will get you to the airport."

"I hope I make it before anything more happens to her. It's a long flight. It's about 7 hours. I need to speak to the doctor in charge before I leave to get more details. If Muriel, the realtor wants to show the house, while I am gone, please ask Collette to make sure everything is in tip top shape." Ann said.

The first flight I could get from Nice to New Haven was five am next morning. I flew out. I thought I would never get there. When I got off the plane, got a taxi, I had the driver to take me directly to the hospital with my luggage. I asked to leave luggage at the front desk. I went to the desk outside of intensive care.

The nurse asked, "What was that name again?"

"I said Marie Anderson." Ann screamed.

"I don't have her on my list. I just came on at two. I will check with the head nurse. Ms. Riley, let me call her. "Is there a Marie Anderson in this unit?"

"I will be there in a moment, Jan." Ms. Riley said.

"Are you Mrs. Durand?" Ms. Riley asked.

"Yes, where is my mother?"

"Mrs. Durand, please come over and sit down."

"No, no I don't want to sit down, I want to see my mother, now!"

"What is your first name?"

"Ann, where is my mother?"

I was beating on Ms. Riley's chest. I already knew that something was wrong.

"Now Ann, I need to tell you your mother went into cardiac arrest, and she failed to come out. Your mother has passed."

"You can't tell me that. I don't believe you. Where is my mother?"

Ms. Riley struggled to hold me in her arms, I continued to pound on her chest.

"Is there anyone who lives in New Haven that I could call for you?"

"Just call my friend Laura. I need her right now."

Ms. Riley got ahold of Laura. She was just leaving for a class at the gym. "I will be there within one half hour or less."

Laura arrived and Ms. Riley filled her in on what was happening. I saw Laura and they tell me I fainted. "I think when Ann saw me, she knew it was for real." Laura told Ms. Riley.

The staff doctor came in and said that Ann would need some medication to get her through.

Laura called Antonio to tell him the situation.

Antonio said, "I feel awful that I left her go alone, but someone had to run Durand. We did not know how this would turn out. How is Ann doing?"

"They have her lying down now, and I will be taking her home with me tonight. She will need a few days rest to get a grip on all of this." Laura said.

"I will do anything I can do from here. I will fly in to bring her back with me. I love her so much. I feel her pain as my own. My parents both died young. I still remember my denial that it could possibly be permanent, Ann lost her father and now her mom. Keep me

posted. Laura, thanks so much for being there for her."
Antonio said.

When I came to some of my senses, I called Antonio.
"My Mom is gone. Please call Hans and Gerard to tell
them where I am. I will promise to call you as soon as
I know more." Ann said.

"Ann, get some rest. I will be there as soon as I can."

"She may want to talk to you more tomorrow. Stay
strong, Antonio." Laura said.

Laura checked me out of the hospital and took me
to her house, she told me. That all is hazy to me as I was
medicated. Laura put me in the guest room and next
thing I knew it was morning. I did not know where I
was as I had never been to New Haven since Laura got
married. She came to see me in Nice, but I never went
to her new house.

She came into my room, and I asked, "Laura, is this
for real. Mom is gone or was it a bad dream?"

"Ann come out for some breakfast. I know you don't
feel like eating, but you need some food. Yes, it is true."

"I need to call Antonio." Ann said.

"I talked to him yesterday and he feels so bad that
he let you to go alone." Laura said.

"He needed to stay to take care of Durand and I
thought I would be back in a few days as soon as mother
was well."

I phoned Antonio. I was numb. I couldn't even cry
yet. I was medicated, Laura told me.

"Darlin', I can't believe Mom is gone. I didn't get there in time. I will never get past this. I need someone to tell me more of what all happened. Dad died of a heart attack too. They said that she came in with a heart attack and then had a second one and that did it. I must talk to Lisa's mom. She was visiting her when she had to go to hospital."

"Sweetheart, I feel ill that I was not there for you. I would like to fly out today, but two yachts are going out today. Caroline from the office helped me with the demands of the clients. I don't know anything like that. Tomorrow I will fly out to you. Put Laura on the phone a minute." Antonio said.

"Laura, thanks so much for taking my place today. I can be there late tomorrow. Please take care of my Ann."

"I wouldn't be any other place. Ann has always been like a sister to me." Laura said.

Lisa's mom called and came over to check on me.

"Ann, I want to share with you; we were at the restaurant having lunch and your mom seemed not to eat much. She put her hand to her chest and said she felt tight, and she felt nauseous. She was dizzy. I called 911 and on the way to the hospital, they told me she had had a severe heart attack. I followed the ambulance. The ambulance attendants assured me that she was unconscious for the whole ride, she did not know her situation. I hope that is some comfort to you." Lisa's mom said.

She then left and nothing she said could make it better. I needed Antonio.

"Ann, it's time for you to take your pill and I will give you a warm blanket and you can lay on the sofa and rest as you can." Laura said.

Antonio arrived Thursday in the late afternoon and tried to console me. Even Antonio couldn't make it better. He held me and it felt good. Words weren't needed. The next day I had to make arrangements for the cremation, no service as I was the only one left in our family. Antonio had to get back to Durand and keep the home fires burning as the two new guys, getting used to their new responsibilities needed some supervision.

I had to fly to New York and close the apartment. Mom's friend got the word, contacted me and met me at the apartment. He told me his name was Tim and my mother and he had been seeing each other for the last six months. He was crushed at the news too. Lisa's mom had called him.

"Ann, your mother spoke of you often. She loved you so much. She was a special lady and we loved each other. I am sorry for the circumstances we are meeting. She wanted to keep our relationship private as you now see, we are twenty years apart. Your mother was vibrant and youthful for her age. It seemed as though we were the same age in many ways." Tim said.

"Mom never mentioned you, but if she loved you, I accept you, Tim."

My mother never mentioned him. Maybe she didn't want me to know as he was a lot younger than mom. Tim said that he would take care of closing the apartment. I told him if mom loved him, I would trust him to dispose of her things. I gave him permission to handle it all, as he was willing. I found her metal box with all her paperwork in it. She was an organized person.

I spent the afternoon going through paperwork and making calls. She had thousands in her checkbook and there was a Vanguard acct. I found her last statement. She had several million in investments. She had money from when my dad died and then inheritance from my grandmother and her own money. I could work on the rest when I would arrive home.

Chapter 32

ALESSANDRO FOUND
A PROPERTY

On Monday I flew to Nice. I was glad to be back with Antonio. My healing process would take some time.

"Ann, whatever you need, I am here for you. I cannot take away your pain, but I will support you in every other way. Collette is going to prepare dinner here tonight. I know you will need a lot of rest. She is making Stuffed Manicotti tonight. I know that's one of your favorites."

Antonio sat on the sofa with his arm around me and covered my legs with the afghan. He sat quiet, exactly what I needed. No words would help, but he is always comforting to me. I love him so much. He is such a gentle soul.

The house was rather still this week. Collette didn't talk much, and Antonio was super busy trying to get Durand ready for Anthony's company to take over.

Alessandro found a property he thought was perfect for us. Antonio told him about my mom, and he understood it was difficult for me to think right now. He sent pictures and when I saw them, even in my grief, I already saw possibilities in the outer building for my Human Library. The property was on the edge of town. People could get there easily. Capri was the perfect place. The people there would love this new concept. It was a relief to think about something for us right now.

Antonio said that it would be a short drive to Aldo's restaurant for him.

Chapter 33

CLIENT FOR HOUSE

*M*uriel, the realtor called and said that she had a client to see our property tomorrow. I had to keep going as much was happening all at one time. It was the man who was being transferred to Nice from the US and he had to find a place by end of September.

The appointment was for one o'clock. Muriel and he arrived about 12:45. Antonio came home, and we left for the two of them to look over the property. Muriel said that they would tour the house and property and call us to answer any questions which she could not. The client and his wife had only a few days in Nice to find a place. He already was in an apartment here, but his wife was only here until Tuesday.

Muriel called about 2:00. "We have finished the tour and they would like to meet the two of you tomorrow at 3 to ask their questions and see if there is any negotiation on a few things. We agreed to the meeting.

Monday at three, we all met.

Muriel introduced us. "Antonio and Ann, this is John and Marilee. They are from New York."

"My mother lived in New York City. She recently passed."

"We are sorry that you have to be selling your house at this sensitive time." Marilee said.

"Thank you. You are considerate." Ann said.

John addressed Antonio with his questions. He seemed to want to deal with a man. I could already tell from how Marilee reacted to him, in his household, he had the say.

"John, you need to speak with Ann as she is the owner of this property." Antonio said.

John was visibly taken aback. I was self-assured enough to ignore his arrogance and carry on. I felt sorry for Marilee. Too bad she wasn't strong enough to deal with him.

After answering all his current questions, they said they would get back to us, either later today or early tomorrow as Marilee's flight would take off at 5pm. They left.

"Antonio, what do you think about it?"

"I don't really know, only thing is, John is under the gun because his wife probably won't get another trip here. A company will generally pay for only one trip for a spouse."

"It would be a miracle if our sale went that fast. First couple to see it and take it. I am not counting on it yet." Ann said.

Next morning, Muriel called. "John and Marilee have called their financial advisor and talked with him and want to come over and make an offer."

"Antonio can not be here until one o'clock. I will want him to be here."

"They will be fine with that. As you know Marilee's flight is for 5." Muriel said.

I called Antonio at the marina, and he said that he would be here.

One o'clock and they arrived.

"Bienvenue," Ann said.

"Come in and we will sit at the dining table." Antonio said.

They knew the house just went on the market and felt we would take a quick sale, I thought.

Muriel started. "The offer is 677 million."

"I don't consider that a fair offer, but I will make a counteroffer. You know we are asking 777 million. My counteroffer is bottom line 700 million. Final." Ann stated.

"Could we be left alone for a few minutes?" John asked.

"Certainly, Antonio and I will be outdoors on the veranda. Muriel can come get us when you are finished." Ann said.

About half hour later, Muriel called us in. They agreed at 700 and they and we agreed October 1 move in date. We shook hands as I stood in disbelief. I thought finally one thing went right for me. They signed the deal. I really needed something to go easier. We wished Marilee a safe flight and they left.

Muriel came back in for a minute and said she would talk to me in her office later in the week.

"Darlin', I really need to go lie down for a while. This day was exhausting. My head was spinning. Everything was a blur."

Antonio reached for my hand and said,

"Come with me. I will lie down with you, until you doze off. Here lie down and I will put a blanket over you, so you don't get chilled."

Chapter 34

THE PERFECT PLACE?

I heard the phone ring,
"Antonio it's Alessandro." Collette called.

"Antonio, I think this property is a perfect place for you to live. It is right on the water. It has four bedrooms, four bathrooms, an office space and is only four miles from Aldo's restaurant. The property is on the edge of town and there is an outbuilding. Ann might want to run her Human Library from there. I wish you could come see it before it's gone. It is the one I had mentioned to you before."

"I would have to speak to Ann about it. She is feeling exhausted right now as her mother passed, and she did not get there in time to see her before. She did not know it was that serious, but it happened quickly. I

will call you if I feel Ann would be ready to discuss it."
Antonio said.

I woke about four and Antonio was sitting out on
the veranda.

"There you are sleeping beauty of mine. Feeling
better now?"

"Oh yeah, I felt so tired. It is beautiful out here. I
want to eat out here tonight. The air is wafting from all
the flowers. Who was on the phone? I thought I heard
it ring or was I dreaming?"

"It was Alessandro." Antonio answered.

I called to Collette, "Can you come out a minute
and bring some lavender water?"

Collette brought out some macaroons and the
pitcher of lavender water with two glasses.

"Ann, I love you so much, I wish I could take your
pain away. All I can do is to hold you, I love you, and
support what you need. I will try as I can to keep things
at Durand in order. I will need you with me at the end
of this week as John wants to stop over here and look
one more time so he can call Marilee and refresh her
memory on what she saw. She was only here once and
has some questions." Antonio said.

"I will do best I can, but you do understand how
devastated I am right now."

"Sweetheart, I will be here for you always for whatever you need. I would like to tell you what Alessandro

and I talked about today when he called. Would that be alright?"

"Darlin', I am a big girl, and I will have to compart-mentalize my thinking. We have many decisions that have to be made right now, so shoot, what's up?"

"Well, Alessandro has seen the property that he thinks fits us perfectly. It is on the edge of the city. It is only four miles from the restaurant, and it has an outbuilding that Alessandro thought might be for your Human Library. It's the one he talked about last week. He is concerned it might be sold."

"Antonio is it possible for you to fly there and see it? I trust you know what we like. I would take care of Durand while you were gone."

"Ann, I really would want you there with me. This is a big decision and I certainly want you to make the decision."

"Give me until tomorrow as I must make several calls to settle my mother's business affairs and I will try to make arrangements to go, for at least a few days. I would want a few more properties to look at so if we don't take this one, we could see a few others. Time is of the essence as John and Marilee will want this house."

I didn't sleep well these days. I had been through almost more than I could bear. Deaths come in threes, they say, and I guess I just went through that with Claud, Andre and Mom.

It was a busy day Friday, making calls, calling Caroline at the office to make sure everything was copacetic. Antonio came in the door and said that Alessandro wanted to encourage us. He thought the property fit us that well.

Chapter 35

FLIGHT TO CAPRI

"Darlin', I will fly out Monday with you. I can only stay until Thursday because I have a major client, very demanding wanting all kinds of props for his yacht trip. He wants to be sure there is enough Dom Perignon and if they run out to get a seaplane to deliver more. He wants a bevy of beautiful women to accommodate his male companions. They need to have been tested clean and be willing to attend to their guests fetishes. The client, I told him would have to pay appropriately and he agreed."

He said, "Just handle it, understand?"

"Please schedule a flight Monday late as I have a whole day of work that I need to do before I go." Ann requested.

Antonio and I didn't speak much on the flight as I dosed off. I was totally in la la land these days.

Alessandro met us at the airport, and he had arranged to see the property first thing in the morning. We stayed at Alessandro's that night. We had a lovely dinner prepared by his beautiful young lady friend, Greta. It was a great Lasagna, Antonio and Egidio's favorite.

The property was for sale by Christies International. The agent Rafael was congenial.

I was astonished at first glance, looking down at the bay. The villa stood high on the property. It was three stories, all white. Styling was European. The architecture had so many curves. It had balconies off all three levels with white wrought iron curved railings overlooking the sea. The view was breathtaking. The outer areas had all upholstered red sofa and chairs. The walkways were all inlaid grey stone. There was a grove of shade trees with metal filagree table and chairs, several with red umbrellas. It had four bedrooms and four bathrooms.

Rafael allowed us to stroll through and around for some time. He then came and took us out to sit in the shade of the Cypress trees. We sat around the table, Antonio, Alessandro and I. Rafael brought a bottle of Barbera red wine. Each of us had a glass and Rafael was ready to answer our questions. I had a little trouble understanding him. I now was fluent in French, but not so in Italian. Antonio on the other hand was raised in the early part of his life in Sicily so he was fluent. Sometimes he had to explain the conversation. Rafael was bilingual but, I still needed some assistance from Antonio.

He answered all our questions and then left us alone again as by now, he thought he had a deal. It was unbelievable. Everything we could want was there and we did not feel to look further. It was like a miracle; however, Alessandro had looked at several places for us as he lived in Capri. He knew us well. We had given him a list of what we needed. Alessandro did well for us.

We promised to get back to Rafael the next day. Alessandro had made reservations at Lo Smeraldo. Aldo sat us at the chef's table with him. We talked a lot about how our life seemed to fall in line, near perfectly, other than my mom's passing. Aldo was anxious to have Antonio come to Capri. My impression was that Aldo would step down as soon as he had Antonio trained. I felt Antonio would like it that way too as he was not used to being second. Dinner was outstanding. Each of us had seafood entrees. When you are on the Mediterranean, it's a must to enjoy fish, shrimp or mussels.

After dinner the five of us went out onto the veranda. We each had a glass of Campari. The guys were talking about Antonio and the restaurant and Greta and I were talking about my ideas for the Human Library. She was not familiar with the concept. I explained the idea was initiated in Denmark and was expanding. Instead of loaning out a book at the library, you would be loaning out a person for one half hour. You would pick one of the topics of the day and choose a person. Examples of topics could be victim of sexual assault, deaf and blind, a person of color and many others. The idea is to get a better understanding of topics you know nothing or little about. She had been living in Italy most of her life and she thought Capri would be a perfect place for the human library.

We called the night early as we would need to meet with Rafael in the morning. Antonio and I talked in our room until late because we already loved the place. It seemed perfect. It was rather pricey, but money was never an issue. Antonio had plenty of money on his own, but I always wanted to be independent and have my feet solid on the ground, so I insisted the deed be in my name only with Antonio as the beneficiary. He was uncomfortable with the idea. He said that he wanted to contribute, however, I said that he would need the money to buy out Aldo if that would come up as I pictured it.

"If this all goes down, I would have you on the restaurant deed as the beneficiary." Antonio said.

"Darlin', I think we agree on most things. Sometimes I think we were married in another lifetime. We think so much alike."

Chapter 36

FINAL OFFER

*W*e decided to make an offer on the property with Rafael. This property was so unique that it would take a special client to like it, afford it and they would have to be in good shape to get up and down the many paths down to the water.

We offered 6,350,000. The asking price was 7,000,000. Raphael looked displeased.

I spoke loud and clear. "I am leaving today at 5pm. I am not coming back. I have a company to run. This is not only my offer, but also my final offer, Raphael."

"I will have to make a call. I will be back here in a few."

Raphael sauntered back. "Ann and Antonio, you will be the new owners of "Le Chateau."

"We will need to finish paperwork today as I said, I need to leave and be at the airport by 3:30."

Raphael left to go back to his office and said that we could meet him there at 2pm.

"Ann, I have to tell you, you have balls. I never saw a woman make a deal so quickly and do it so well. I never want to be on the wrong side of you. As I know you personally, you are a powder puff, sweet and gentle, but when you go into your business mode, Wow! I really am impressed by your proficiency." Antonio said.

"My grandmother, whom I spent a lot of time with, when I visited her in Paris gave me good advice. She told me, "Don't play your Ace first. Hold your cards close to your vest. If you know you are right, use your big girl voice. Use your soft voice when you want to show kindness. Hold on to your values and principles. Wise woman.""

"Ann, you must have listened well. I love all your many facets. I never know which one is going to show up."

We said goodbye to Alessandro and Greta and Alessandro drove us to the airport to return home.

When we arrived home, Collette told us that Anthony had called several times. Now what, I thought. I called him immediately and he answered.

"Ann, we are wanting to acquire Durand on September 1 rather than October 1."

Anthony, I will need to call you back tomorrow. That's a huge change, four weeks earlier."

"I need to know as early as possible."

What I did not know at the time, Ms. Balencia, his mother was pressuring him as her birthday was coming in early September and she wanted control of Durand and not to have to deal with me. Anthony had to do whatever she said because she held the purse strings.

I planned, because now we had a buyer for the house and we already signed a contract for our new home in Capri, we would just as soon turn over Durand early while we are still living here. At that point we could move sooner. I talked it over with Antonio and we agreed. I didn't want to say yes to Anthony at the time, so I appeared to still be in control of the Balencia's.

Chapter 37

BALENCIA PLANS

"Mr. Balencia please. This is Ann Durand."

"He is out of the office but was awaiting your call. I will call him on his cell."

He called back quickly.

"Anthony here, Ann."

"Anthony, it will be tough, however I will respect your request. We will turn the keys over September 1. You will need to get your people or person over here to understand how the company operates." Ann said.

I have a person, Gino who will run the entire company using your people for starts." Anthony replied.

I went to the marina in the afternoon to let my people know, who had become near family to me, especially when Egidio passed. I wanted them to know Anthony possibly would bring in his own people.

I came in the house, threw my purse on the dining table and Antonio was standing there.

"Antonio, I have had it. Without you, I would go back stateside and bury myself in a room. This year has been way too much for anyone to deal with."

"Ann, I am here. The best is being put together. You want to sell Durand. You did. You want to live in Italy. You will soon. You want the Human Library; you will have it. Hang tight, I will support you through this all. You don't need to do this alone. Sometimes I think you try to be too independent. You are not alone, unless you kick me to the curb."

"Darlin', I love you so much. You are always here for me; I do appreciate you. I think when I wasn't there when mom passed, it really pushed me over the edge."

"Come lie down with me. I will hold you and give you a soothing back rub. Just know, I love you. I am here as long as you will have me." Antonio said.

Collette had Ravioli ready at seven. After dinner, we invited Collette to come to the Gazebo with us. She was not used to being with us on a personal basis that much, but I had come to become attached.

She brought down some expresso and macaroons.

Chapter 38

COLLETTE, WILL YOU COME?

"Collette, I know you don't have much family, I have a proposition for you. I would like you to consider moving to Capri with us. The contract would give you three weeks a year vacation with an airline ticket to come back to Nice to visit whom you choose. We would be paying you monthly, considerably more than you make now. Think it over and get back to me in a few days."

Collette went quiet. She said nothing. I had no idea what was going through her mind.

"Ms. Ann, I will let you know as soon as I can."

She picked up the empty cups and did not come back.

"Antonio, I am attached to Collette, I feel like I am her mother. Her parents are not alive. She never wanted to talk about it, I left it alone."

"It would be good to keep her. Many times, they know how to clean only and she on the other hand cooks. I know you don't care to cook or clean up."

"Darlin', that's why I spend my time with a chef. You enjoy cooking. I like eating. We are good together."

Next day Collette came to me and she had a smile on her face.

"Ms. Ann, I have carefully decided. I talked to my aunt. She lives in Genoa and said she would come visit sometime. She agreed with my thought, how much I enjoy being with you and Antonio and I like the job."

"Collette, would that be a yes.? You know I love you as part of my family" Ann said.

"Yes, I would love to go with you. When will we be going?"

"Quite soon. The business is sold, the house is sold, and we decided on a new home in Capri. I will show you some pictures soon."

Antonio came in and asked, "What's for dinner, it smells good?"

Collette was preparing Chicken Parmesan. She is such a treasure as she has a special touch to all her cooking.

After dinner, Antonio and I went to sit at the water. It was a warm breezy evening, and the sun was setting.

We had each brought our drinks along. I glanced over at Antonio.

"Darlin', you will never know how much you mean to me and every time I see you in that white shirt with the top buttons open and see your dark hairy chest, I want to go to bed. You are in for a great night ahead. Let's have an early night."

He reached out his hand and said, "I don't have to be convinced, let's go now."

We adjourned our party to our room. He threw the covers back, he undressed me and I turned out the lights. We made love for hours as Antonio knew how to treat a lady.

"Good morning, my love. I brought you some juice, fruit and a baguette, and here is your favorite tea. Thank you, sweetheart, for a beautiful night."

I was rubbing my eyes, half awake, and Antonio was up and running; that is one thing we are different. I like to sleep in, and Antonio is an early riser. I had to come to, to say something wonderful after all he did and said, so I figured, I can't go wrong with, "I love you more than you will ever know."

Okay, he hopped in the other side of the bed and began putting strawberries in my mouth one at a time. My eyes caught his and my heart was full of warmth and joy. I was content with him at my side. I began blinking and giving him butterfly kisses on his cheeks.

Chapter 39

MOVE TO CAPRI

*T*oday we really had to put our fast-moving life in order. We showered and started our day. The move was scheduled in three weeks. We hired a moving company to do all the packing as well as the move. Antonio had dealt with Anthony and his people to make a smooth transition of Durand. I was dealing with the realtor in Capri as to any details. There were some minor repairs to the home we agreed on. I needed to make sure that everything was done. The realtor was so on top of things that she said the home was move in ready. All cupboards were already wiped out and the movers would be able to unpack immediately.

Finally, my life seemed in order, Mom's estate was settled, and she had left everything to me as I was the only one left. I have such a wonderful partner.

Moving day came. Antonio and I had laid out a plan, where in the new house each piece of furniture would go, I stayed here to supervise the move and the movers would arrive at the new house on the next day. Antonio went ahead to Capri and stayed at Alessandro's, and I would fly out after. I would meet Antonio at Alessandro's.

Friday, I flew out and the two of us directed the movers. It went smooth as we had planned. The movers Caroline suggested were best bar none.

That evening, Greta cooked dinner for us so we didn't have to go out. We stayed at their house that night and in the morning, we went and dressed the beds and whatever we needed to move in. Collette stayed with a friend that weekend and I arranged a ticket for her to come on Tuesday. I wanted to hire someone to replace Pierre. We needed a gardener/driver. Greta used a fellow a while ago that she said was recently available, so I called him.

He was great and I agreed to hire him with a caveat that if for either of us it didn't work, we would talk. His name was Mario. I asked him to pick up Collette at the airport. He and Collette were about the same age. I thought they would work well together.

The first week was hectic. We had our room and then Collette and Mario had to decide which bedroom of the two choices they each would have. Collette had first choice and picked the room with the larger bath. Mario wasn't fussy. He was just happy to be with us and have this new job. We had a car for our driver and told Mario he could use it on off times with permission from either of us. He told us that he had overseen the lawn care and grounds at Giardini di Augusto, the botanical gardens near Capri.

Saturday night, we met at Lo Smeraldo with Alessandro, Greta and Aldo. After dinner, Aldo, Alessandro, and Antonio took a tour of the restaurant property. Aldo suggested to Antonio that he would only want to be an advisor and Antonio should run the restaurant.

"Aldo, I will have to digest this all. I came to work for you, but I didn't know you meant in that way."

"I know you are capable in so many ways, Antonio."

They came back to meet Greta and I in the lounge. It was a pleasant evening. Greta was interested in helping me start up the Human Library that I was planning. She had been a teacher in her career. What a fabulous happening for me.

Right from the get-go we loved our new home and were glad we had made this decision. Collette and Mario were getting along well. As we did before Collette and Mario ate in the kitchen and Antonio and

I ate in the dining area. It appeared not only did they work well together, but Mario had eyes for Collette. She had long dark hair and big brown eyes and a great figure. She, when working kept her hair pulled back. She had creamy smooth skin.

It was only a month and Antonio was loving working at Lo Smeraldo. Aldo didn't even come in much anymore. The staff and Antonio hit it off from day one. He had had experience dealing with different staffs at all the restaurants where he had been chef.

Chapter 40

ALDO IS IN HOSPITAL

*A*lessandro called the restaurant one day and said that the hospital called him. He was on Aldo's chart who to call if needed. The nurse suggested he come to the hospital. Aldo was not doing well. He went directly to the hospital. Aldo was sleeping all the while Alessandro was there. He was on a machine to breath. Antonio was beside himself when he heard this and insisted to go to the hospital the next morning.

The next day Antonio and Alessandro went to see Aldo. The nurse said that it would only be a day or so. Aldo was rarely conscious. He was able to barely talk, but when he heard Antonio's voice, he seemed to rally.

"Antonio, I did not want to tell you, but I have had lung cancer for quite a while. That's why I wanted to preserve my company. I worked hard with it. I want you to keep it going. I have it in my will now to leave it to you. I don't have much time, but I feel good now to know it will live on through you, my friend."

Within the hour, he closed his eyes, and the monitor went off. That was it. He was gone.

"I am so glad we made it up here to see him and let him speak and rest in peace knowing his company will still live on." Antonio said.

They left the hospital and Antonio came home. He looked pale.

"What's the matter Antonio? I can see you are distraught." Ann asked.

"It's Aldo. He passed at the hospital as we sat with him. We never knew he had lung cancer. He never told us. He told me at the hospital. In his will he left the restaurant to me. Wow, it's difficult to express how I feel."

"Darlin', you need to grieve and rest right now. I know you will take care of the restaurant well. I will hold you and be there for you as you have been for me always. You have known Aldo many years. It hurts. I know hurt so well, so often."

Antonio had to hit the ground running on Monday. The restaurant was closed, but Antonio called the employees in and had to tell them the news and allowed them to absorb, he now was their boss.

Antonio and Alessandro made plans for a memorial service. He was to be buried next to his wife who died five years ago. They had two plots. They had no children.

Antonio and I paid for it all as we felt appropriate.

The following week, business had to go on as usual and Antonio had to double time it. He had been in the restaurant mostly himself so that made it easier. No wonder Aldo was rarely there, breaking in Antonio to take over.

Chapter 41

LA REVE

W e sat out on the veranda one evening having a drink. It was a beautiful evening. There was a breeze off the sea. The sunset was serene.

"I am thinking of changing the name of the restaurant to Le Reve, "The Dream." I have, way in the depths of my mind wanted to own a restaurant. I would want to assign one of the people who already work there to manage the restaurant. I still want to be the Chef and have a sous chef. I want to be with you as much as possible so the sous chef could take up the slack. I know you will be busy with your library too."

"Antonio, it is time we now can each live our attainable dream. It's just you and I now. We love each other and I see us together for the foreseeable future."

Chapter 42

SPECIAL SATURDAY NIGHT

"Ann, I want us to have a Special night this Saturday to celebrate. I want to take you to Gennaro Amitrano. Get on your Sunday best and I will too. They have only about six tables. It is all French service. We deserve it."

"Darlin', it sounds wonderful. I love you."

Saturday night, I came out of the bedroom. Antonio insisted, "Twirl for me. You look like a fairytale come true. That dress is dynamite, only because you are inside of it. What stunning shoes. Come here and let me hold you before we go."

I had gone shopping with Greta to Via Camerelle and Carré d'Or. My dress was a strapless, black chiffon. It was fitted in the body with a flair at the hem. It

149

moved when you moved. I had black spikes with gold shiny heels. My necklace was a thin strand of diamonds, Egidio had given me for our anniversary.

Antonio was in a black pinstripe suit with a black shirt. His hair was beginning to turn. It was now salt and pepper, made him even more attractive.

Mario was dropping us off and would pick us up tonight.

We arrived at the restaurant and as usual Antonio's reputation followed him. We were immediately led to a quiet intimate private corner of this secluded space of ambience.

Antonio ordered a bottle of Dom Perignon. We toasted each other to living our dream.

Dinner was amazing. I ordered Scampi and Antonio had Octopus. After dinner, Antonio reached for my hand and led me to the lounge area. It had modern white leather seating and the area had soft lighting in darker blues. The whole area was a sea of dark blue lighting. The room was filled with romance. Antonio asked the waiter to bring us Tiramisu with two forks and each a cup of expresso. It was decadent. He raised his fork to my mouth, and I fed him. We were the only ones in this blue seclusion. Suddenly as we sat on the sofas, Antonio laid his fork down, bent down on one knee in front of me, pulled a small box out of his pocket, opened it and asked," My love Ann, will you marry me?"

I was so surprised; I didn't answer right away, and he looked shocked.

"Oh yes, oh yes for sure. I love you with all my heart."

He reached for my hand and as he put the ring on my finger and said," Sweetheart you are my Day and my Night, my Summer and my Spring. I love you until infinity. I cannot imagine my life without you."

We kissed and hugged and then I first really looked at the diamond. The stone was a Marquise. The ring sparkled even in the low lighting. My feet never hit the floor the rest of the evening. I was in ecstasy. Antonio had planned next to go to VV Club Capri to dance. We took a taxi there and danced until late in the evening.

We called Mario to pick us up and arrived home about 2am.

Next morning, Antonio kissed me on the forehead to awaken me. He had a tray on the table in our room. I put on a robe, and we sat on the loveseat, and we enjoyed fruit, baguettes and tea. I propped my hand on the Kleenex box on the table to stare at my ring. As the sunlight came through the window, my ring created rainbow sparkles all over.

Antonio just watched me keep looking at the ring with a full smile on his face and a sparkle in his eye.

"Did I surprise you?"

"Of course not, you silly goose." I said laughingly.

"Wow, our life has been on speed dial lately, all good though." Antonio quipped.

After breakfast, I was going to get my notebook that I left in the office. As I went down the hallway, I glanced and saw Collette coming out of Mario's room. Interesting, oh well.

Chapter 43

HUMAN LIBRARY

I needed to make some calls today to meet with several people who might help me with setting up the Human Library. Greta was coming over. She wanted to know more about this new idea.

Greta came in the afternoon, and we sat out on the veranda at the table, and I explained the concept to her.

"Instead of you taking books out of a library, you get to spend a half hour with a human versed on a certain subject. Each day I will have a list of about six topics. There will be six volunteers with expertise on their subject. The client will pay to listen and ask questions of the expert."

"What topics are you expecting to cover, Ann?" Greta asked.

"The topics will depend on which volunteers are available on a given day. There will be a schedule. The topics I plan to solicit are, an alcoholic that went dry, a gay person, a transgender person, a divorced person, an author. So, there will be new topics as I can obtain volunteers. I will be holding the library in and around our outer building on our property. I will need to advertise after I set it up. You, Greta will certainly be an asset. The area with the Cypress trees will allow shade and I will have benches and separate areas for each group to meet. The areas need to be separate so each group cannot hear the other."

"I am excited to be a part of your new venture. What will you name it, Ann?

"Its name will be, Garden of Understanding, learning to unjudge."

"Beautiful, Ann." Greta commented.

Greta left about four and Antonio came in the door.

"Hello there my future wife." He smiled and kissed me on the forehead.

"How was your day? Ann asked.

Chapter 44

BIRTHDAY JOY

"Really uneventful. I heard someone is having a birthday this weekend.

"I wonder who?"

"I couldn't guess."

"I would like to have dinner here Saturday evening. I will cook for you. This is a special birthday number."

Saturday night, the lights were turned down low, candles were lit everywhere. All red candles, all sizes and shapes. Red rose petals covered a path to the table. The table had a red cloth draped to the floor. Ivory tall candles were on the table. A bouquet of white cymbidium orchids was in the center of the table. Collette and Mario had the night off. Antonio had a bottle of Champagne. He had prepared Filet Mignon, parsnip hash, mixed vegetables with a sprig of parsley. Collette was off, he did this all for me, himself.

"Darlin', I feel so special."

"Sweetheart, you are my special angel. I love you to pieces."

Dinner was wonderful. And then Antonio brought out dessert. He brought out Strawberry crepes with mounds of vanilla ice cream and myriads of whipped cream. He picked up his fork and filled my mouth with ice cream and strawberries. I took my fork and fed him.

"I have this card for you, and I want you to read it out loud." Antonio requested.

I was overwhelmed, but in a state of euphoria.

"Ann, I want to fulfill this card for you." Antonio said.

"Okay if you say, I will read it aloud."

It read, My birthday wishes for you, I will,

1) Splash champagne over all your body
2) Massage you in lavender oil
3) Serve you cheese and crackers
4) Serve you chocolate covered strawberries
5) Take you to the hot tub
6) Move to the boudoir
7) Slither your robe to your feet
8) Reach for your hand and toss you on the bed
9) more to come later"

After dinner and dessert, Antonio led me to the bedroom.

"Let the love continue. I will read the rest of the evening from my heart." Antonio promised.

We had let the directions from the card unfold and now Antonio was in charge.

"I will lavish kisses and indulge your entire body. Landing at the center of your castle door until you are totally satisfied and then enter your castle. Then I will hold you until you fall off to dreamland." Antonio whispered.

He turned the lights off. A beautiful birthday. Probably the best birthday ever, Antonio was a beautiful person as well as a perfect lover.

Morning came and as he often did, Antonio kissed my forehead and had my breakfast on a tray.

Life could not be more beautiful. Antonio and I decided to get married and go to Figi for two weeks for our honeymoon. Our life was now near perfect after the many twists and turns it had endured.

9 781662 835063